The Thurston

Heirloom

The Thurston Heirloom

A Thurston Hotel Novel
Book Nine

Suzanne Stengl

Publisher: Mya & Angus
Cover Design: Su Kopil

www.suzannestengl.com

MYA & ANGUS

Dear Reader,

The Thurston Hotel is located on Main Street in the mountain resort town of Harmony, Alberta. Built by Thomas Thurston, the hotel opened in 1916. His three grandchildren—Wendy, Bailey and Ben—operate the six-story hotel today.

The town and the hotel are fictional, but the actual location is not. Working as a group, we found it was helpful to know our surroundings, so we chose beautiful Canmore, Alberta as our setting. Tucked in the foothills of the Canadian Rockies, Canmore is just outside the gates of Banff National Park.

The Thurston Hotel Novels are stand-alone romances connected by the Thurston Hotel and the town of Harmony.

Each book represents one month in 2016. I am the "September" book. Several plotlines overlap and one recurring plotline begins in the January book and hopefully ends with a wedding in the December book.

For more about the books and authors of this series, check out our website at www.ThurstonHotelBooks.com. There's even a map of Harmony.

Since 1916, the hotel's motto has been, *We promise you'll enjoy your stay at the Thurston.*

Happy reading!

Suzanne Stengl

Dedication

To Mrs. Arbuckle
who held the team together,

and to all the Thurston authors
and their wonderful imaginations

Chapter One

For almost an hour, the mountains had been nothing more than a narrow band on the horizon as the Greyhound Bus cruised west along the Trans-Canada. On this first day of September, the air was warm and the sky was clear. Twenty-eight years old, Jill-of-all-trades and recently dumped by her fiancé, Mariah Patrick had boarded the bus this morning at half past seven.

Rumpled and cramped, she adjusted her position, trying not to disturb the old man sleeping in the seat beside her—her companion for the whole trip, and he hadn't spoken a word. She'd said hello, twice, and he'd ignored her. Maybe he was deaf.

Bald on top, his well-trimmed white hair ringed his head and contrasted with his dark eyebrows. He was clean shaven but for a salt and pepper mustache. And he was sleeping, which was why she could study him now.

He wore a navy blue sports jacket of good quality, a pale blue shirt with a fine stripe design and a button down collar, open at the throat. A pair of gold-rimmed spectacles perched on his nose.

Besides that, he had a ruddy complexion, laugh lines around his eyes—even as he slept—and a content expression. He looked like a retired businessman who had made a good decision and was reaping its benefits.

She had made a decision too, a short week ago. That was when she'd decided to leave town. An easy decision, considering there wasn't anything or anyone keeping her in Fort Mac. She didn't even have family there. But then, she didn't have family, period.

And, of course, there were the dreams.

Turning away from her sleeping neighbor, she glanced out the window again. The mountains were closer. Very close, in fact. After traveling all day, they went around the bend and were now completely surrounded by mountains.

She hadn't known it would feel like this. She'd never seen mountains up close and personal, and pictures didn't do them justice. The massive peaks of the Rockies rose up all around the highway, like enormous and powerful creatures, like guardians who watched over the world, who put everything into perspective, and who made everything right.

As if that could happen.

She laughed at herself, and touched the medallion, pressing it against her heart. As always, she wore the medallion under her clothes where no one could see it.

The road wound past a place called *Lac Des Arcs*—a small, crystal-clear lake—with some kind of industry on the north shore. Industry, so they were not inside the National Park. Not yet.

Then, a few minutes later, they passed another highway sign that said *Dead Man's Flats*. An odd name, but . . . at least it was colorful. Had they named it to attract tourists? Or had it always had that name?

The bus barreled on, leaving lesser vehicles in its wake, until at last, the signs announced the town of Harmony, Alberta. Population 12,000.

Harmony. A familiar name, now. The name she'd heard in her dreams for the past few weeks, repeating like a mantra, compelling her to finally leave the only home she'd ever known, and start life over.

. . . . .

Teague Farraday, businessman, owner of Mountain Jewel Sports, and mountain guide—mostly mountain guide—backed his pickup truck into the loading zone at the Greyhound Terminal.

His shipment of ski boots waited for him along with some alpine merchandise: fleece vests, woolen socks, trekking poles, sleeping bags, tent pegs and bear bells. For some reason, the tourists liked the bear bells.

With any luck, he'd be out of here and back at the store before the new kid ran into problems. At least his longtime employee, Monroe, knew what he was doing, but the new kid was taking a while to train. Hopefully he'd work out because the store needed help.

And Teague needed to get out of the store and into the mountains. Guiding was what he liked doing, not fitting ski boots and coordinating colors for jackets and helmets.

He shrugged the ache out of his shoulders, and the concerns out of his head. It had been a long day, starting over twelve hours ago, and he needed a break.

With shadows slanting, the clock neared half past seven. The sun would set in an hour. The town would be dark by nine, and it would be time for the store to close. The tourists would give up their spots in front of the store's fireplace and put their coffee mugs in the dishwasher. They'd take one last glance at the maps on the Tours Table, sign out a hiking book, and then wander off to find other things to do, leaving him to restock shelves. Not his idea of an exciting night but it had to be done.

Maybe he could get Monroe and the new kid to stay late. For now, he'd better get this stuff loaded. He jumped out of the truck, turned toward the platform, and heard someone call him.

"Hey, Teague!"

Jason Knight—his friend, and favorite bartender—stood near the taxi stand. The hotel must have given the man time off. Or, more likely, he was here to collect someone at the terminal.

"Jason! What are you doing here?"

"Mrs. A sent me to meet the bus."

Of course she did. Mrs. Arbuckle often sent Jason on errands, and Jason didn't seem to mind. In fact, judging by everything he'd seen, Jason liked the old girl. "Someone important showing up?"

"Apparently." Jason glanced down the street, looking for the bus.

"Who?"

"No idea. She said I'd know when I saw them."

That's what Mrs. Arbuckle would say, he thought. "Most people hold up a sign."

"Too easy." Jason laughed. "Besides, it's probably a test. You know how she is."

Teague did know. She was eccentric, wealthy, and probably harmless. "Some bigwig from the city?"

"Your guess is as good as mine."

Still no sign of the bus. "As long as you're waiting, want to give me a hand?"

With Jason's help, they had the shipment loaded into the bed of the pickup by the time the Greyhound lumbered into the terminal. Curiosity won over concern for the new kid and the store, so Teague waited with Jason, wondering who the important guest was.

Standing side by side, they leaned against the truck, arms folded, and watched as the Greyhound came to a stop, the air brakes hissed and the door folded open. Charlie Gallagher stepped down, headed for the baggage compartments and lifted the hatches.

Not a tourist bus, obviously. Otherwise Charlie would have stood there and helped the passengers to disembark.

Charlie drove the route from Calgary to Kamloops. He'd be here about an hour, pick up more travelers and then continue west. Now, with all the baggage compartments open, and the passengers offloading, Charlie joined them by Teague's truck.

"No tourists?" Jason asked.

"Maybe a few, some kids with backpacks," Charlie said. "Most of these folks have been traveling all day, down from Fort Mac."

Looking for new jobs in the small tourist town, Teague guessed. After the wildfires last May, a lot of people had to relocate.

The three of them stood and watched the assortment of passengers step off the bus. A group of teenagers with backpacks, a middle-aged couple with rolling suitcases, two old ladies with small bags heading over to get a cab.

Teague recognized a bartender who worked in the Peaks Bar at the hotel. The guy stepped down, followed by one of the maids. They'd probably spent their day off in the city.

Next came two young girls with long straight brown hair and winning smiles. "There they are," Teague said. The girls popped down the stairs, each wielding about a half dozen brightly colored shopping bags.

"The twins?" Jason sounded disappointed. "That's it?"

"That's enough," Teague said, glad that at least Mrs. Arbuckle worried about them. Their mother didn't seem to.

Roberta Smythe tended to ignore her thirteen-year-old twins, but Reba and Dolly didn't seem to mind. Whenever Teague saw them, they were polite, happy and oddly well-adjusted. Maybe because they had each other.

It must be nice to have someone who was always with you.

Jason made a move to intercept the twins, and stopped. "Drop by the bar tonight," he said. "I'll give you a beer. On the house."

"I don't think management likes that." But Teague laughed, knowing how Bailey kept a vigilant eye on things over at the hotel.

"Perks." With a broad smile, Jason held up both hands like he was catching something from the sky, then he jogged over to the girls, gathered a few of the shopping bags and led them to his car.

Time to return to the store. Besides the restocking, Teague needed to look at the books and get the paperwork done. Thinking about it filled him with dread. He'd sooner stab himself with a teaspoon than do paperwork. What if . . .

With an impulsive thought, he pulled out his cell and dialed the store. Monroe answered on the first ring. "Send the new kid over to the bus station. He can drive this stuff back and unload it."

"Right away, Boss."

Pausing, Teague gave himself one last moment to change his mind. And then, "Can you lock up tonight?"

"Sure thing."

Monroe rang off, and Teague felt a moment of gratitude. Monroe liked dealing with the customers and he was good at it. Teague was fortunate to have the guy.

Decision made, he felt lighter already. His plan was to catch a ride with Jason, grab some dinner at the hotel, and then kick back at the bar. He turned to tell Jason to wait, but something made him glance at the bus again and . . . his breath caught.

A young woman wearing an orange jacket and a small blue day pack held onto the bus railing as she managed the three deep steps. She staggered as her foot touched the ground. No doubt, she was one of the passengers who had made the long trip from Fort Mac.

Mesmerized, Teague stood next to his truck, unable to

move. He'd never seen anyone so beautiful in his life. She had reddish brown hair, and lots of it. Creamy white skin, and tired eyes. And there was something else. He felt as if he were looking at someone he'd known for a long time . . . but, he didn't know her.

She was about five foot seven, same height as Bailey. In fact, she even looked a little like Bailey. Then, on second thought, not at all like Bailey. Whereas Bailey shouted confidence, this woman looked lost and alone, like the person who was supposed to meet her had not shown up.

She plodded over to the baggage compartment, dropped her day pack on the ground, and tugged on a large blue duffel bag.

And then the new kid showed up. The ever eager Shredder McGee. "Hey, Boss." Shredder's chest heaved as he caught his breath. The store was across the street, on the other side of the gas station, but the kid must have run all the way, probably hoping for points. Teague handed him the keys.

Happy to be useful, Shredder climbed into the truck, started the engine and revved it unnecessarily. He gave Teague a salute and took off. At least he hadn't skidded the tires.

Turning back to the woman, Teague felt that sense of déjà vu again. Of course, he'd never seen her before, except for her strange resemblance to Bailey.

By now, she had the blue duffel on the ground and she'd clipped her day pack to the top of it. The duffel had wheels, otherwise she'd never be able to move it, even as far as the taxi stand.

Reaching into the compartment again, she pulled out a folded garment bag—silver with loop handles on either end—and she placed it on top of the duffel.

Still frozen on the spot, he stared at her. Then, giving himself a mental slap, he straightened his shoulders and approached, arriving as she hauled one more piece of baggage from the compartment. A large backpack. Not large for him, but definitely large for her.

"Need some help?" he asked.

"No thanks," she said without looking at him.

"What?"

"I said, no thanks. I've got it." This time she did look at him, briefly.

Up close, he could see her blue eyes. "Are you sure?" Deep, dark blue, like a mountain lake at sunset.

"I don't need any help."

She looked like she needed help. But somehow she hoisted the backpack up onto her shoulders and fastened the belt. Then she picked up the garment bag by its loops, grabbed the handle of the duffel and headed for the street.

"Taxi stand is that way," he said.

"I can walk."

And she could, slowly, moving like an overburdened packhorse. She stepped into the street, heading toward the gas station on the other side. She must have a ride waiting there.

But, she walked past the gas station. Dumbfounded, he crossed the street and caught up with her as she reached Mountain Jewel Sports, his store.

"My truck is behind this store."

"Sure it is." She kept walking.

"It is. Go into the store—See that store?" He pointed to the door.

"The jewelry store?"

Jewelry? What was she talking about? "It's not a *jewelry* store."

She paused and looked up at the sign he'd commissioned last year. Then she kept walking.

"Jewel," she said, sounding distracted. "Mountain Jewel is pretty, but the *Sports* needs to be larger. It gives the wrong impression."

He stopped walking, turned around and looked up at his sign. She might have a point. But everyone knew this was Mountain Jewel Sports. So what if the *Sports* was in small lettering?

He ran to catch up with her. "Everyone here knows what it means."

"Everyone who lives here. But I expect a lot of that store's business comes from tourists," she said. "Who do not live here."

Again, that made sense. "Never thought of that," he said, unconcerned. "Why don't you let me carry that pack?"

She stopped and faced him. "Are you stalking me?"

"No, I'm trying to be helpful." Then he added, "You're not making it easy."

"I don't know you."

"You don't have to know me. This is a friendly town. Everyone knows me."

But not only did she not know him, apparently she didn't want to. She walked away, heading down the street with her heavy load.

He stopped walking and let her carry on alone, wondering where she was going. And, more important, wondering what the hell was he doing.

The fact was, she knew exactly where she was going, and it was most likely close by. Not only that, she was probably meeting someone. Some lucky guy who for whatever reason had not shown up at the depot.

What an idiot.

Rubbing his hands over his head, Teague thought a moment, and decided. It made sense to follow her. To hang back and make sure she didn't collapse. Because she sure looked like she might.

Chapter Two

The stranger had taken her mind off her problems, temporarily anyway. Reluctantly, she had to admit he was cute.

More than cute. Tall, and achingly handsome with light brown hair and clear blue eyes. He spent hours in the sun, judging by the sun-bleached strands that peppered his hair. And yes, she had been rude to him, but it was the only way she knew to protect herself. Continuing her university courses, finding a decent job and rebuilding her life, that was her number one priority.

Not getting to know some good-looking guy with a gorgeous smile. He probably had a string of broken hearts all around this town and she was not going to be one of them. Not going to happen. It would take a blue moon before she went down that path again.

Right now she needed to find that hotel she'd Googled.

Standing at the curb, she waited for some cars to pass. The small town didn't have a lot of traffic, but it had steady traffic, probably a combination of tourists and locals.

From what she'd read on the library computer, the hotel employed a large staff, so there had to be some kind of work there. She could wait tables, she could work at reception, maybe she could even get a junior position in their accounting department since she'd already completed two of the accounting courses for her degree.

And she had to find a place to stay, hopefully before it

got dark. But not to worry. This was a tourist town, between summer and ski season. Surely there would be some accommodation available? Some place that didn't require a deposit? At least until she could get her first pay check.

She stopped in front of a store that said *Spirit Song Books and Gifts.*

Bending her knees, she lowered the duffel to the sidewalk and dumped the garment bag on top of it. An ache pulsed along her spine. She adjusted the belt of the backpack, trying to shift the weight so it didn't hurt so much.

That turned out to be a useless endeavor. All she could really do was get to the hotel as quickly as possible. It would have been nice to take a cab, but spending money on a cab was out of the question.

If only the Internet connection at the library had been more reliable, she might have seen some pictures of the hotel. As it was, all she knew was that it was located somewhere on this Main Street of Harmony. And she'd better find it soon, because she didn't think she could carry this load much longer.

For the first time since this fantastic plan had taken hold in her mind, she began to doubt herself. Because, now that she was in Harmony, the impulsiveness of her decision amazed her. She didn't do impulsive. She thought things out, made plans, followed checklists.

But the urge to leave Fort Mac and move here had been so strong she couldn't resist it. All in one week, she'd signed off on her job with the cleanup crew, she'd collected the few things she had left that had not been destroyed by the fires, and she'd used every last cent she had to clear her debt. Especially the debt with the caterers and the hall.

The thought of that almost-wedding still sent a shiver through her. But no matter, it was over. With everything paid for, she'd ended up with enough money for a Greyhound ticket south and a peanut butter sandwich.

On the street, a car braked suddenly, another car honked its horn and whizzed past. Life rushed on in the small town.

Carefully balancing the backpack, Mariah picked up the garment bag and the handle of the duffel, and inched down the street toward the next intersection, a T from the left, with a tall building on her right, on the south side of Main. The old brick building was six stories tall, but she couldn't see the entrance. It must be around the corner.

Hoping this was the hotel, she crossed to the south side of the street, and that's when she saw him. The old man who had sat beside her on the bus.

He stood at the far end of the building, on the sidewalk, wearing his navy sports jacket and waving his arms as if he were cheering her on. Mariah looked around to see if he was waving at someone else, but no, he seemed to be waving to her. Peculiar.

Feeling like she was moving in slow motion, she trudged on. The old man disappeared around the corner of the building and she followed, until finally she could see the impressive entrance of the Thurston Hotel with its sandstone brick and its expansive steps—steps that were flanked by black lampposts each with five white globes. And, over top of the gabled portico, were the three flags representing Canada, the USA and the Province of Alberta. Everything about that entrance was welcoming, and familiar.

An odd sensation echoed through her body. She'd never seen the Thurston Hotel in her life, but something about it made her feel like she was coming home.

She shook her head to dispel the silly thought. The explanation was simple. She must have seen a picture of the hotel in a brochure at the Travel Center in Fort Mac and the image had stuck in her memory.

By now, the old man had gone inside. A bellhop in a black uniform stepped out of the door. And suddenly a ball of white fluff—a little dog—came racing down the stairs and along the sidewalk in her direction, heading toward the street.

A car blasted its horn.

. . . . .

When he'd seen her stop to adjust her load, it had taken all his willpower not to rush ahead and offer his help—again. Of course, it would have been useless, since, for whatever reason, she didn't want help.

Then suddenly, he saw the dog. And, in one motion, he saw her drop the duffel and garment bag, click the release on the pack, slip out of it, and dash into the street. She scooped up the little dog, stumbled back across the curb and rolled onto the sidewalk.

The car skidded to a stop.

Gill reached her a moment before Teague did.

Letting go of a tight breath, he started to breathe again. She was safe, nothing had happened, except for a tear in the sleeve of her jacket.

Gill knelt beside her. Teague stood on her other side. He glanced at Gill, saw the relief register. A close call.

Cradling the dog in her arms, she murmured something calming. The dog licked her face, and she laughed.

She laughed! How could she laugh? It was a musical sound, and it intrigued him, and annoyed him at the same time. She could have been hit trying to rescue Mrs. Arbuckle's stupid little dog.

"Is she okay?" The driver of the car stood on the sidewalk. "I wasn't driving fast. Last thing you expect is a dog to run out in front of you."

"He's okay," the woman said, referring to the dog.

"She," Gill corrected her. "This is Betty Jo, but most of us call her Killer."

And usually they only did that when Mrs. Arbuckle couldn't hear them. "Killer needs a leash," Teague said.

The woman was staring at him, no doubt recognizing him from the bus depot, and no doubt wondering why he was here—following her.

"I don't know what happened." Gill got hold of the dog's collar. "One moment I was clipping on her leash, then the lights flickered and I couldn't see her." While the woman held Killer, Gill attached the leash. "The hotel probably needs new wiring."

"They upgraded the electrical last year," Teague said. "Could have been anything. Doesn't matter. Are you all right?"

"I'm fine, really," the woman said, speaking to the driver of the car. "It wasn't your fault. Thanks for checking."

The driver, an older man, grinned like he'd won a prize and this beautiful woman had presented it to him. "Is that your stuff?" he asked, indicating the pile of baggage on the sidewalk. The duffel with the day pack, the backpack, the garment bag. "Can I give you a lift somewhere?"

"Thank you," she said. "But this is where I was going."

The hotel? Why was she going to the hotel? Wouldn't a hotel guest have taken a cab?

"We'll carry her stuff," Gill told the driver. He handed the man a card. "This is for you. Bring a friend. It's good anytime."

The driver thanked him and left.

"What was that?" Teague asked.

"Mrs. Arbuckle would want him to have it. It's a free dinner for two in the Foothills Dining Room."

"How do you know?"

"It says, right on the card."

Sometimes Teague wasn't sure if Gill was serious or not. "I meant, how do you know she'd want to pay for dinner?"

"I know," Gill said. "She'll be so happy her Betty Jo wasn't hurt."

Teague knew how much the eccentric Mrs. Arbuckle loved her dog. As the stories went, she had loved Mr. Arbuckle too, right up until he'd died five years ago. That's when the old lady had moved into the hotel. Now she lived in one of the top-floor suites and ruled over her domain. As far as he could tell, she was a benevolent ruler.

Gripping the leash, Gill set the dog on the sidewalk. Then he slung the garment bag over one arm. "I'll pull the duffel, Teague. Can you get the backpack?"

"No, don't help me. I'm not a guest. I'm looking for work."

"Doesn't mean we can't help you," Gill said.

"But I—"

Ignoring her protest, Gill left, with the garment bag, the duffel and Killer.

Teague lifted the woman to her feet, and kept hold of her elbow.

"How's your arm?"

"It's fi—" But then she saw the tear.

He separated the fabric on her sleeve to get a look. Her beige sweater had also been ripped. "Your elbow is scraped. I'll bet Mrs. Arbuckle will want to feed you too."

"I don't need—"

"Of course you don't. Can you walk?"

She tested her balance, and seemed okay. He let go of her elbow, made sure she was steady, and then picked up the backpack. A heavy load. He slung it onto one shoulder, surprised that she could have lifted it.

He would have waited to walk beside her but he expected an argument, so he went ahead. In a few minutes, they were all inside the hotel.

Gill had set the duffel and day pack in front of the reception desk. He'd also folded and placed the silver garment bag neatly on top. The way he would for any guest.

Teague approached the desk and, too late, he realized Roberta was working tonight.

"Teague!" she called to him, in a voice full of enthusiasm. "What are you doing here, honey?" Then, with a puzzled tone, "Are you checking in?"

He supposed it might look that way. He lowered the backpack beside the duffel. "I'm helping Gill," he said.

Today, Roberta Smythe was a slightly darker blonde. The same puffed up hair, the same dark eye makeup. The same predatory look.

Glancing back, he saw the woman from the bus depot push through the doors, and he noticed how her orange jacket suited her reddish brown hair. He really needed to get her name.

A touch of anxiety traced over her tired expression. Along with that, and her torn sleeve, she looked like a waif blown in off the street.

She unbuttoned her jacket, and then, absently, she cupped her injured elbow. Walking slowly, she entered the lobby, then stopped, and stared, at everything. The high ceilings, the textured walls, the blue and gold brocade of the carpeting, the broad staircase leading up to the second floor and the ballroom.

She was awestruck. The Thurston Hotel did that to people.

Gill had found Mrs. Arbuckle in her usual spot across from the reception desk. Here, a trio of red velour wingback chairs circled a glass pedestal table. On the table, a silver tray held a pitcher of cream and a bowl of sugar cubes. Two white teacups ranged on either side of the tray.

Mrs. Arbuckle liked to sit in this spot and talk to the

hotel guests, acting as if she were one of the hotel owners. From her vantage point, she could see the reception desk and anyone who came through the front doors.

Tonight, Mrs. Jamieson sat beside her. Mrs. Emily Thurston Jamieson really was one of the hotel owners. In fact, she'd been the manager of the hotel right up until August last year, when she'd had a heart attack. And, judging by the way she looked right now, she might be having another one.

That, or she'd seen a ghost.

At any rate, Emily Thurston Jamieson, with her normally porcelain skin and white hair, was decidedly pale. Sitting in the wingback chair, she held her hand tightly pressed against her heart. Gill had better make sure someone accompanied her back to her retirement residence.

Or, wait a minute, maybe the paleness had something to do with Gill telling them the story of Killer's near miss with the car. And knowing Gill, he was embellishing the story.

"I'm looking for a job."

Teague turned back and saw his bus depot woman at the reception desk talking to Roberta.

"I'm sorry, honey," Roberta said.

She used her professional voice, knowing that Mrs. Jamieson was in earshot. Otherwise she would have told the transient to leave.

"There isn't anyone here to talk to you now," Roberta continued. "It's after eight o'clock."

Teague watched the interplay, saw Roberta's pleased expression—the one that said she held all the power at the hotel tonight.

"Check back in the morning," Roberta said, with a dismissive tone. "There may be someone who can see you then."

Hearing that, Mrs. Arbuckle jumped to her feet and marched up to the long mahogany desk. "They were short a maid this morning," she said. "I heard Bailey talking about it. And there's that couple coming for their honeymoon, and the Andersons are here."

"I'm sorry, Mrs. Arbuckle," Roberta answered, with a note of condescension. "You're not authorized to hand out jobs on the spur of the moment."

"Miss Smythe is correct." Mrs. Jamieson rose from her seat. She looked vibrant and healthy again. No sign of her earlier bout of paleness.

Roberta beamed at Mrs. Jamieson, and sent a smug look to Mrs. Arbuckle.

"Mrs. Arbuckle can't make any hiring decisions," Mrs. Jamieson confirmed. And then, after a second's pause, she said, "But I can." And then Mrs. Jamieson, *the* Mrs. Emily Thurston Jamieson, took charge and turned to the bus depot woman.

"What is your name?"

The bus depot woman stood tall, shoulders back, head up. "Mariah Patrick."

Mrs. Jamieson's mouth dropped open, then she swallowed. It seemed as if her composure left her again.

She should really sit down, Teague thought. He would have suggested it, but he knew all about Emily Thurston Jamieson and he was not about to offer her advice. She did not suffer fools lightly.

"Patrick," Mrs. Jamieson repeated, in a whisper. "Yes, that's the name." She spoke quietly, almost to herself, and hesitated.

Again, Teague wondered if she was all right. But in the next instant, she resumed her interview.

"Would you like to do housekeeping here?"

"Yes, I would."

"Do you have any experience?"

A slight pause. "No, but I learn quickly."

"Very well. You're hired."

Mariah Patrick smiled, a full beautiful smile like the sun had come out from behind the clouds and all was well with the world.

"You . . . you're not from around here?" Mrs. Jamieson asked, apparently not done with her interview.

"No, I arrived on the bus, about a half hour ago."

"From?"

"From Fort McMurray."

"I see." Another short pause. "How old are you?"

Not prepared for the question, Mariah Patrick waited a beat, and then answered. "I'm twenty-eight," she said.

Mrs. Jamieson stared at her. "I thought you looked young." She frowned. "Do you have any siblings?"

"Any—" Mariah Patrick tilted her head slightly. "Pardon?"

Yes, Teague wondered. What did siblings have to do with this interview?

"Any siblings?" Mrs. Jamieson persisted. "Any brothers or sisters?"

"No," Mariah answered, looking confused by the question. "Not here. Not anywhere."

Mrs. Jamieson nodded, slowly, looking lost in thought. Then she snapped out of it and continued questioning. "Do you have a place to stay?"

"She can have the apartment above my store," Teague said, trying to be helpful, and perhaps being a bit selfish.

"Or she could stay in the staff room," Roberta volunteered. "In the basement."

No doubt Roberta had extended that generosity because she didn't want competition. She didn't like the idea of this beautiful woman being anywhere near him.

"There are only cots down there," Mrs. Jamieson said. She stared at the floor, thinking. Then she asked, "Is anyone else staying there, Miss Smythe?"

"No, ma'am. Not at the moment."

"Good." Mrs. Jamieson turned to Gill. "Give the dog to Mrs. Arbuckle."

After Gill handed over the dog, Mrs. Jamieson said, "Bring Miss . . . Patrick's luggage to the staff room. Miss Smythe, leave a message for Tessa. She will do the orientation in the morning."

Orders issued, Mrs. Jamieson turned to Mrs. Arbuckle. "Maddie," she said, sounding tired. "Let's go to the Thomas Lounge. I need a drink."

"I'd better put Betty Jo back in my suite." Mrs. Arbuckle cuddled the little dog. "You know how Jason doesn't like her in the bar."

"Don't worry about Jason. You can bring your dog in for the time being." She turned to Gill, who was picking up the duffel. "Gill, when you're finished with the luggage, come and get the dog."

Chapter Three

Breathing a sigh of relief, Mariah watched as the two matrons left the lobby and drifted down the hall, presumably toward the Thomas Lounge. The old gentleman, the one from the bus, followed behind them. And then, he stopped, turned around, and winked at her.

She nodded and sent him a smile, wondering if he'd had anything to do with her getting the job so quickly.

"Let me show you where you'll be staying," the bellhop said.

He was a young man, younger than she was, and he wore a black uniform with dark green trim. A two-way radio was clipped on his belt. Mrs. Arbuckle's friend had called him Gill. And that other man? The one that had followed her from the bus depot? The bellhop had used his name when they were outside, when she'd been sitting on the sidewalk holding the little dog.

"Teague? Can you give me a hand?" Gill asked, picking up the handle of her duffel bag.

Teague. His name is Teague. And this is Gill. And that's Mrs. Arbuckle. Mariah filed the names in memory.

"Sure," Teague said, lifting the backpack, effortlessly, and slinging it onto one broad shoulder.

Mariah gave her head a little shake, trying not to think about broad shoulders. Broad shoulders didn't matter. But she needed to learn her employer's name, that mattered. Except no one had addressed the woman by name, and

Mariah had been too intimidated to ask. No doubt, she'd find out soon enough.

And then there was the old gentleman from the bus. No one had called him by name, or even spoken to him but, somehow, it seemed he was a regular visitor here in this hotel.

The woman behind the long dark mahogany desk, that was Miss Smythe. Right now, she was staring at Teague, with doe eyes and come-hither looks.

"This way," Gill said, heading back toward the entrance and the service stairs behind the valet station.

Mariah glanced up at Teague. He inclined his head, indicating that she go first.

Gill wheeled the duffel as far as the stairs, and then picked it up to carry it down. She could have at least unclipped her day pack and carried that much, but he didn't give her a chance. So she followed Gill, and Teague followed her.

One flight of stairs later, they reached the basement floor. On either side of the stairs, closed doors were marked as *Meeting Room 1* and *Meeting Room 2*.

Ahead, on the right side of the hall, came the sound of pans clattering—the kitchen, still in full swing with the evening meal preparation.

Gill set the duffel down, picked up the handle and wheeled it to a room on the left side of the hall, across from the kitchen.

He flicked the light switch and went inside. Mariah followed, in time to see him disappear through an interior door, probably the room with the cots.

She stood in the doorway. To her right was a kitchenette consisting of microwave, two burner stove top, sink, dishwasher, fridge and an assortment of cream-colored cabinets. To her left, a large round table accommodated four comfortable chairs, and beyond the table was the interior door. Straight ahead, a row of tall green lockers took up the whole wall.

With a sudden fluster, she realized she had stopped in the doorway. Teague stood behind her, still shouldering the heavy pack. "Sorry," she said, moving farther into the room.

He looked at her, lifted an eyebrow, as if he didn't understand what she was sorry for. That made sense. He could probably hold that pack all day and not notice the weight.

He walked past her and into the room where Gill had gone. In half a minute, they both returned.

"We put your things on the floor," Gill said, with a crooked smile. "I'll get you a lock and you can stow anything you want in here." He tapped his hand against one of the green doors. "Like Roberta said, no one else is staying down here now, so you'll have the place to yourself."

"Roberta?" Could that be how he referred to their employer?

"The receptionist," Gill said. "The blonde at the check-in desk."

Mariah nodded. Miss Smythe was Roberta to the lesser staff.

And who was Teague?

Outside, on the street, he had looked tall. In the small room, he looked even taller, much taller than Gill, who was probably an inch taller than she was.

Unlike Gill, Teague wore no uniform so he wasn't staff. And, judging by the way he was helping, he was a friend of Gill's. Was he a friend of Roberta's too? Or a past lover?

Or a current one?

It didn't matter, Mariah knew. The important thing was Teague was not her friend and couldn't be. Not at this point in her life. Not after all that had happened with that failed wedding. *Not going to do that again.*

"I don't suppose you'd like to have dinner with me?" Teague asked.

She almost laughed. The guy wasn't used to *no* for an answer.

"To welcome you to Harmony." He shuffled his feet, and actually looked shy.

It was a gracious invitation, and she was tempted to accept it. The man was charming, and friendly, and handsome. And exactly the sort of man she needed to keep away from. "No thank you."

"The Foothills Dining Room is upstairs," he persisted. "Lots of people."

"I said, no thank you."

He closed his eyes briefly, accepting her answer with a grimace. "Fine." He marched quickly to the door. Then he stopped and turned to Gill. "If she asks, tell Roberta I went home."

"Are you going home?" Gill asked.

"I'm going up to the Thomas Lounge. By the far stairs," Teague said, and after one last glance at her, he left.

Still standing beside the green lockers, Gill waited, with his head tilted, as if he were listening to Teague's footsteps echo down the hall. When the footsteps were far away, Gill laughed. "He likes you."

"Pardon?"

"He likes you. And don't worry, Teague's a good guy. You should give him a chance."

So the comical little bellhop was a matchmaker? "What if I already have a boyfriend?" *What if I have an ex-fiancé who is still messing up my head?*

"Then you should get rid of that boyfriend and go out with Teague." Gill said it simply, with a friendly grin.

Mariah didn't know how to answer.

"Did he say something to piss you off?"

Not exactly. And she would never admit she was attracted to him. All the more reason to keep her distance. Her life did not need complications. Besides . . . "He followed me from the bus depot."

Gill shrugged. "Probably wanted to help you with that load." He slanted his head, thinking about it. "He offered and you said no. Right?"

Was she that obvious? "Right," she admitted.

"Like I said, he's a good guy. Don't worry about him."

"I'm not interested."

"Sure," Gill said, agreeing with her, but not meaning it. "If you need anything, I'm on duty until eleven tonight. Come up the service stairs and you'll find me." He touched the two-way radio on his belt. "Or get Roberta to page me." Then he bounced out of the room, like he didn't have a care. Before she could even thank him.

Rushing to the door, she saw him at the foot of the stairs. "Gill?"

He turned and faced her.

"Thanks for everything."

"No problem." He skipped up the stairs and was gone, leaving her alone, for the first time on this long day.

A wave of tiredness hit her. The adrenaline rush of arriving, catching Mrs. Arbuckle's little dog, getting a job almost instantly.

Now that she thought about it, having her employer in the lobby tonight had been a stroke of luck. It was like having a fairy godmother in the hotel. And maybe an evil stepsister, in the form of that desk clerk.

But, to be fair, Roberta either was in a relationship with Teague, or wanted to be. The woman must think Mariah was competition.

That misconception would have to be cleared up. For now though, she needed to see where she'd be sleeping.

A moment later she stood at the doorway to the

interior room. Straight ahead were two cots against the wall. To her right, along the exterior wall, was an egress window and two more cots. And to her left, tucked behind the door, was a single cot. That would be hers.

The cots had low wooden headboards and footboards, white linen folded down, two pillows each, and red bedspreads. Two white towels topped each bed.

Was there a shower anywhere?

She found it a minute later—in the room past the staffroom. It was a small bathroom with vanity, toilet and shower stall at the end. A hot shower would feel so good, but first she needed something to eat.

Returning to the staff room, she considered the fridge. Could there possibly be any food in there?

She opened the door, and let out a long disappointed sigh. There was nothing but a can of coffee and a box of baking soda. A search of the cabinets revealed dry coffee whitener and sugar cubes. Maybe, she could eat the sugar cubes . . . Chasing after that thought was the one where she reconsidered Teague's offer of dinner.

No. She'd done the right thing. She was not going out with anyone again. Not until she had her life under control. And even then, she wasn't going out with anyone like him.

Especially not like him. He was too handsome, too tall, too in charge. Too much.

A tap on the door announced Gill's return. He held a cafeteria-size tray in his hands. "From our chef, Guy Lafontaine," he said, setting the tray on the table.

There was a huge whole grain bun, with thick slabs of roast beef, and melting white cheese. Lettuce and slices of tomato poked out from under the top half of the bun. Also on the tray were a wedge of pumpkin pie and a tall glass of milk with moisture condensing on the glass. She wanted to bolt it all down at once.

"Tell Guy thank you."

"You'll meet him tomorrow," Gill said. "You can tell him yourself." He plunked a lock and key on the table, and disappeared.

She considered the lock for a moment. She could put the garment bag in one of the lockers. Not that she cared if it was locked up.

Hardly able to believe her good fortune, she sank into a chair, picked up the sandwich and took a bite. Tender roast beef, Swiss cheese and that was . . . yes . . . it was horseradish.

This completed her day. This strange day that somehow felt like coming home.

She would eat, she would shower, then she would sleep. Tomorrow she would meet that Tessa person and get the orientation for her housekeeping job. At some point, she'd have a break and she'd find the library. The library would have a computer, and she would continue her online courses.

Touching her sweater, she felt the medallion underneath and pressed it against her heart. Everything would work out, she told herself. Somehow, it would all work out.

· · · · ·

When Teague had entered the bustling Thomas Lounge, there had only been one place left at the bar—the seat next to Mrs. Arbuckle, who was sitting beside Mrs. Jamieson.

The two old ladies huddled together, having one of their *discuss the state of the world* conversations. So deep in conversation, they didn't notice him. Not that either of them ever took much interest in him anyway.

Fortunately, Gill had come for the dog and taken it back up to Mrs. Arbuckle's suite.

"I've told her she can't bring her dog in here," Jason said, in a low voice as he leaned across the bar.

"I know." Teague saw the distress on Jason's face. Jason was an easy going guy. He didn't like to make waves, but rules were rules.

"Mrs. Jamieson said it was all right, and she should know better," Jason said. "I may have to talk to Ben."

Ben Thurston, Mrs. Jamieson's nephew, and the current manager of the hotel. "Do you think it would help?" Ben really didn't need to know about the dog.

Jason huffed out a sigh. "Probably not." He shrugged and let it go. "Your order is almost ready."

"Thanks."

Teague settled back in his chair and watched the bar, glancing every once in a while at the two old ladies beside him. Mrs. Jamieson trusted her nephew but she still kept a careful watch over the hotel. And Ben, he was calmer these days, ever since he'd got married. The guy had learned to relax a bit. Before he'd met Melanie, he'd been on course for a heart attack himself.

"Jason?" Mrs. Emily Thurston Jamieson, using her imperious voice, called the bartender. "Another Baileys and cream, please." As soon as she'd put in her order, she turned back to Mrs. Arbuckle and their conversation.

The Thomas Lounge pulsed with activity tonight. Jason handled orders with his usual efficiency. The servers worked the room, appearing relaxed and chatty, but hustling when they moved. It was almost nine o'clock so things should settle down soon.

"The age isn't right," Mrs. Jamieson said. Her voice had grown louder, as she'd quaffed more Baileys. "She would have been at least four years older."

"So maybe Mary wasn't pregnant when she left." Mrs. Arbuckle sipped her drink.

Her customary vodka on the rocks with a lemon wedge.

She wouldn't call it alcohol. It would be her *medicinal* before bedtime.

"Then why did she leave?" Mrs. Jamieson lamented.

Teague wasn't trying to listen in, but Mrs. Jamieson kept getting louder and she seemed disturbed by whatever they were talking about. Although, for all he knew, they were discussing a soap opera.

"Because *you* told her *not* to," Mrs. Arbuckle answered. A tone of "I told you so" lacing her words.

So, maybe it wasn't a soap opera. Maybe it was some drama they'd bought into when they were at their hairdresser's. The two of them needed some amusement.

Feeling a tap on his shoulder, Teague turned around.

Gill had returned. "I brought her the food. Told her it was from Guy."

"Thanks," Teague said. "I owe you."

"No, you don't. I owe you for saving my skin on that kayak trip."

"You would have been fine. Don't worry about it."

Gill made a move to leave, then stopped. "You like her," he said, with a grin.

"Get out of here."

The bellhop headed back to his post and Jason returned with Mrs. Jamieson's drink—the Baileys and cream, and Teague's dinner—a steak sandwich and fries. Jason pushed the ketchup and salt and pepper close, and then he was gone again.

"What I don't understand is why Mary didn't come herself," Mrs. Jamieson complained.

"Probably afraid of her welcome," Mrs. Arbuckle said, patting Mrs. Jamieson's hand.

"But why send her daughter? And then not tell her about me?"

Jason reappeared with a cold bottle of Rickard's Red, popped the top and slid it next to the plate. "Roberta's asking about you."

Teague resisted the urge to look over his shoulder. Somewhere along the line, Roberta had decided the twins needed a dad, and he was her current target.

"She's not here," Jason said. "She called from the front desk, to see if *you* were here."

"What did you say?"

"I sidestepped. I said I'd seen you, at the bus depot."

"And that distracted her?"

"Yeah. She thanked me for giving the twins a ride back to the hotel. I think she forgot they were in the city today."

"She's a great mom," Teague said, meaning she wasn't. Reba and Dolly were good kids, but somebody needed to keep an eye on them.

"I suppose they're learning self-sufficiency," Jason said, wiping the bar. "They were probably doing one last city run before school starts."

"School starts next Tuesday?"

"Yep. And this is the Labor Day weekend. It's gonna be busy around here." Jason left to take another order.

It was busy now. And tomorrow, Friday, it would be hectic. Everyone liked to get out of the city for the last long weekend of the summer. The Thurston Hotel would thrive on the business and the staff would be run off their feet.

"She really didn't recognize you?" Mrs. Arbuckle carried on with her chatter.

"How would she recognize me? She's never met me."

"I meant your name."

"Maddie. It's not like anyone introduced me."

Teague wondered how much business would change this year. Today was the first of September and the weather was still warm. But as the cooler days approached, guiding would ease off. There would still be hiking tours for most of this month, then a lull in October and November until the winter sports took over.

"Tomorrow, you can call her to your room," Mrs. Jamieson said. "I'll be there and you can introduce me."

"What if she's busy?"

"I'll make sure she's not. It will be a part-time job."

Jason was back. "Do you think Roberta even knew they went to the city today?"

"Knowing Roberta, I have a feeling she didn't."

"She has you on her radar, you know that, right?"

"Yeah." It would have been hard not to notice. Although, right now, he didn't want to think about Roberta, or even about how to get rid of her. His mind was on the little waif. Hopefully she was well fed and sleeping.

She'd looked so tired and worn out, and broken. And, judging by the way she couldn't afford cab fare, she had no money. For some reason, she'd decided to leave Fort Mac and try her luck in this tourist town.

He'd like to help her, but she had a solid streak of independence. No matter how much he wanted to take care of her, he had a feeling she wouldn't let him.

"Does she look like Mary?" Mrs. Arbuckle asked.

"Spitting image."

"And Mary looks like the portrait in the library?"

"Yes, it's like it's the same person."

Portrait in the library? What the hell were they talking about? And did they mean the town library or the hotel's Margaret Library? Curious, he made a mental note to look in the Margaret Library and see if there were any portraits in there.

"How's the new guy working out?" Jason asked. "What's his name?"

"Shredder."

That got a raised eyebrow from Jason. "That's what he calls himself," Teague said. "Shredder McGee."

"Here to snowboard?"

"So he says."

Jason nodded, thinking about that. "Any good in the store?"

"He's learning."

"Think you can teach him some bookkeeping?"

"Not a chance." He needed someone to come in part time for that. Problem was, most people wanted a full-time position and he couldn't justify full time. Not yet.

He took a long swallow of the mellow beer.

Mrs. Arbuckle set her empty glass on the bar. Then she pinched the lemon, picked it up, and sucked out the juice. "I wonder what happened to the heirloom," she said, dropping the lemon rind back in the glass. "Do you think Mary kept it?"

Mrs. Jamieson swirled her Baileys, watching the ice cubes spin. "She probably had to sell it. She would have needed the money."

"You think so?" Mrs. Arbuckle asked.

A slight pause, and then Mrs. Jamieson said, "That no-account would not have been able to provide for her."

It probably *was* a soap opera, Teague thought, and he tuned them out.

Chapter Four

From a distance, Mariah heard the familiar sounds of ventilators sighing and monitors beeping. An X-ray tech stood beside her, asking for help with positioning a plate, but the patient's IV line was blocked. She'd need to restart it, right away.

She was tapping on the patient's arm, trying to find a vein. Tapping, tapping . . . And suddenly she was in a strange room. No curtains over the window. Dawn.

"Sorry to wake you."

It was a young woman, about her age, wearing green scrubs. But she didn't recognize her. The nurse tapped on her arm again. "You must not have heard your alarm."

"My alarm?"

She'd been dreaming. She'd heard the alarm, and she'd interpreted the sound as the monitor beeping, but it was only the dream. The same recurring dream. Would she ever be able to leave that world behind?

Groggy, she tried to sort out where she was, piecing bits together. The bus trip. The old gentleman who never spoke. The handsome stranger who wanted to buy her dinner. The Thurston Hotel. The job.

The job!

Awareness crashed into her as she fully woke up. "Oh my God. Am I late?"

"No," the woman said with a laugh. "It's six-thirty."

Mariah glanced at the window. "It can't be. It's not light

enough."

"Sunrise at seven," the woman said.

Seven? Not at six-thirty? Then she remembered. She was several degrees of latitude further south. The sun would rise later.

The woman yawned. It must be early for her too. "Brace yourself," she said. "I'm turning on the light." She walked to the doorway, flicked the switch and flooded the room with blinding whiteness. "I'm Tessa. You'll be working with me today."

A loose bun held back her hair, golden blonde with lighter highlights. Her eyes were blue, and her skin was fresh. If she wore makeup, it was very little. She held a stack of green scrubs in her arms.

"I've brought your uniforms. They said you were about my size." She set the scrubs on the end of Mariah's cot. "You get three sets. Every day, you launder one set. The laundry is down the hall, past the bathroom."

Mariah pushed the covers back and sat up.

"Can you be ready in about a half hour?" Tessa asked.

"I'll be quick."

"Good. We'll go for breakfast and then you'll meet Bailey. Bailey Thurston. She runs Accounting here. She'll get you to sign some forms and stuff."

The forms were probably a formality. As for breakfast, it would have to wait. Mariah didn't have any money to spend on breakfast.

"You'll like working here," Tessa said. "The Thurstons are good people and the pay is all right. Not a lot, but you get some perks. We get to have breakfast and lunch for free."

Free food? Mariah's stomach rumbled.

Tessa raised her brows and laughed. "You should see the look on your face. If you love food, you'll love working here."

Mariah felt her face flush. So she looked hungry. So what? She got out of bed to show Tessa she wouldn't be dropping off to sleep again.

"I'll be back in a half hour to get you." Tessa left.

Mariah quickly made her bed, picked up her shower things and a set of scrubs. Except, here at the hotel, this was called a uniform. In a silly twist of fate, the clothes looked exactly like what she'd worn in the ICU.

From ICU nurse to maid. If her mother could see her now.

. . . . .

With the sun shining, no wind, and the cool temperature ideal for hiking, it was the perfect Friday morning for the start of the Labor Day weekend.

Teague watched the tourists boarding the van for their day trip to Lake Louise. It would be an easy hike, the Plain of Six Glaciers. The elevation might be a challenge for a few of them, but nothing serious. And if it was a little more than their usual activity level, they'd have bragging rights in the Thomas Lounge tonight.

Shredder would be sweep on the trail. He would also haul the extra stuff. Extra water, extra sunscreen, blister dressings . . . which they might need. Teague had advised the tourists not to wear new hiking boots, but some of those boots looked shiny.

Hazel Anderson had decided to go on the hike. She lived in Calgary, was staying at the hotel with her husband, and she was Brock Anderson's mother. Apparently they were in town to touch base with their son about his December wedding plans, and to meet Brock's future in-laws.

However, Hazel Anderson, who was probably sixty years old, had never been on a hike before. She wore khaki pants and shirt, a bright red day pack, Oakley sunglasses and one of those Aussie-inspired sunhats that people thought were cool. Around her neck were cords holding binoculars and camera. Shredder would probably be carrying those items before the hike finished.

Hazel's pants were creased, her day pack had never seen use and her boots were shiny. She also had one of those decorative wooden walking sticks they sold at *Spirit Song Books and Gifts*.

"Will we see any bears?" she asked, leaning the walking stick against the van door.

"Probably not." The bears might see them, but the trail had so much traffic, the bears knew to stay away.

"Are you sure I can't bring my bear spray?"

"Yes, I'm sure."

"Why not?"

"Bear spray is a last-resort measure. Avoidance is your best protection."

"But what if we can't avoid them?"

"The bears will avoid you."

"But my husband said—"

"I don't care what your husband said. You're more likely to get hurt by the bear spray than by the bear. People end up spraying it on themselves by accident."

"Is that a problem?" Hazel persisted. Her bear spray had been confiscated and was inside the store. "The bear wouldn't eat you if you were covered with bear spray."

Why did normal, usually rational people think like that? "It could set off an asthma attack. Even a healthy person can have trouble breathing if they get downwind of that stuff."

"But—"

"You'll be traveling in groups and you'll be talking. The bears will hear you and they won't approach."

"But what if I can't talk?"

"You're doing fine now."

"I mean, when I'm hiking. It's hard work. I won't be able to talk."

"If you're working hard to keep up and you can't talk, you're working too hard. You'll need to slow down."

She frowned, still not quite persuaded. "But I don't want to hold anyone up."

"You won't. Everyone will fall into their own group."

"But what if—"

"And Shredder will be the last person on the trail. The bears hate him so you'll have no problem."

"Hey, Boss," Shredder yelled. "Everybody's loaded. Let's go."

Hazel climbed inside and Shredder rode shotgun. Teague got behind the wheel and wondered how Mariah Patrick was faring at her new job, being a maid for the Thurston Hotel. Though she looked timid and unassuming, and though she'd been grateful for the job, he somehow expected it was a step down from whatever she'd done before.

Bailey would have to hire her, because Mrs. Jamieson would insist. But that wouldn't happen right away.

Bailey, ever protective of her clan, would quiz Mariah before actually giving her the job.

And then he would be able to quiz Bailey and get the story on the waif.

. . . . .

"We usually require a resume," Bailey Thurston said, sounding somewhat suspicious.

Mariah sat across from her in the large office. "Like I said, I don't have any experience as a maid, but I learn quickly."

Probably in her mid-thirties, the accounting manager

had chin-length dark brown hair with a curl in it. Her eyes were light brown—a golden brown—and serious, as she looked over a collection of papers on her desk.

"I understand you're here from Fort McMurray?"

"Yes, I arrived last night."

Bailey leaned back in her chair and folded her arms. "What kind of work did you do there?"

"Most recently," Mariah said, "I worked with a cleanup crew."

Bailey nodded. "And before that?"

"A lot of things." Mariah sat up straight and counted off on her fingers. "I've been a waitress, a store clerk, a babysitter, a nanny, a receptionist." She caught her breath. "I've also done data entry, yard work, snow removal, and hanging Christmas lights."

Bailey's mouth dropped open. "Hanging Christmas lights?"

Mariah couldn't help but smile at the manager's surprise. "It's a lot of fun."

Bailey nodded, uncrossed her arms, and leaned forward. She seemed to think those jobs were respectable enough.

"You're a Jill-of-all-trades," she said, losing some of her suspicion.

"For the time being," Mariah answered. "I want to go to university, when I have enough money. Right now, I'm taking online courses for a business degree."

"Business?" Again, Bailey's expression filled with surprise. "Why?"

"Someday, I'd like to manage a store. I've always thought I might be good at it. You know," she paused, and considered. "Something you just have in your blood."

"I see." Bailey smiled, no longer adversarial. She seemed pleased that they had a common love of business. "Which courses have you taken so far?"

"I've completed the basic Accounting, Economics and

Finance. Now I'm working on Statistics."

"Good," Bailey said, approval in her tone.

"And that reminds me, I need access to a computer to do my course. Could you give me the address of the library?"

"It's close," Bailey said. She wrote on a pad, tore off the page and handed it across the desk.

And, as quickly as before, her expression changed. This time from friendly to frowning. "My aunt seems to have a special interest in you."

"Your aunt?"

"Mrs. Jamieson is my aunt. She used to be the manager of the hotel. Now my brother is."

So that was who had hired her. Mrs. Jamieson.

"How do you know Aunt Emily?"

Mrs. Jamieson is Aunt Emily. "I . . . don't."

Bailey looked as puzzled as Mariah felt.

"Have we met?" Bailey asked. "You look familiar."

Another odd question . "I don't think so. I've never been outside of Fort McMurray, so unless you've visited there . . ."

Bailey shook her head, picked up her cell and checked the time. "No, I've never been there." She shrugged. "I suppose it's one of those cases of lookalikes."

Back to the business at hand, she picked up one of the papers. "Are you happy staying in the staffroom?" she asked, pushing the paper toward Mariah. "Here's what comes off your pay check for lodging."

"That's—" Mariah looked twice at the very small deduction. "That's very generous. Thank you."

Bailey shrugged. "As long as you keep the staff quarters and the kitchen area clean, I'm happy."

In fact, the arrangement was perfect. Mariah didn't need anything fancy, it only cost her a pittance and she didn't need to waste time traveling to work.

"Aunt Emily said this was only part time," Bailey said, reading her notes.

Part time? Last night, it had seemed as if it would be a full-time job. But, no matter, it was a start.

Bailey grimaced. "Yesterday, they said they needed a full-time maid and now it's back to part time." She tapped her fingers on her mouth while she mulled that over. "Do you have a preference for hours?"

"Whatever works for you."

"I'll keep you on full time for the Labor Day weekend," Bailey said. "Is that all right?"

"Perfectly."

Speeding along, Bailey went back to her papers. "We're having some special guests." She skimmed a list of names, trailing her fingers over the page. "The Andersons have already arrived. Bill and Hazel Anderson," she said, tapping the names. "They're the parents of a local lawyer, Brock Anderson. He's getting married this December and the reception is in the Diamond Ballroom. They'll be checking out the wedding plans. And, they'll meet his future in-laws." To herself, she mumbled, "That should be interesting."

Then back to Mariah. "We also have a couple showing up for their honeymoon. They'll be in the honeymoon suite on the fourth floor." She flipped a page over, made a note. "It will be the usual treatment. Roses, champagne. Don't worry about it. You'll be working with Tessa. She's used to this stuff." And then, again, she mumbled to herself, "Though why people want rose petals on their sheets is beyond me." She picked up another paper. "Sign here. And here."

Having passed the test, Mariah filled in the blanks. Gradually her life would return to normal. She'd have this part-time job. She'd find another. She'd find the library and carry on with her online courses.

In her mind's eye, she saw a handsome and charming

man. Blue eyes, sun-streaked hair, friendly smile. Obviously, trouble to avoid.

"We're done," Bailey said. "Meet Tessa on the third floor."

. . . . .

The morning flew by. Working side by side, Tessa and Mariah filled the cart with linens, towels, toiletries and writing supplies.

Today was mainly routine cleaning. "Most of the deep cleaning is done when we're not so busy," Tessa said, as she stacked towels embroidered with the green TH monogram.

In each room, they emptied wastebaskets, vacuumed, sanitized the bathroom, dusted and polished furniture, and changed bed linen. They also replaced one light bulb. By one o'clock they both were ready for a break.

"The coffee shop will have emptied out by now and the staff will be getting lunch. It's the daily soup and sandwich, plus coffee. No choice, but it's always something tasty."

Mariah still had to thank the chef for last night's meal. And never mind last night, she'd thank him for lunch, *and* for the excellent breakfast of bacon and eggs too. Gill had mentioned his name last night. "The chef is Guy something?"

"Guy Lafontaine," Tessa said. "He's the executive chef. Pam Sheridan is sous chef. She works the day shift."

Mariah made a mental note to find them and thank them both.

A tiny thought welled up inside her. What if she had said yes to Teague's invitation? Would it have been so terrible? It's not like she could fall in love with the man on the spur of the moment.

Although, there'd been a lot of spur of the moment decisions lately. Best to stay away from Teague.

They left their cleaning cart in the basement, climbed the back stairs to the main floor and were about to head down the hallway, when Tessa paused. Leaning close, she spoke quietly. "See those two?"

Mariah saw a tall young man, about Teague's age, talking with an older native woman.

"That's Nellie Blackbird. She runs the Gift Shop," Tessa said. "I won't introduce you now, since she's busy. But if you happen to need any toiletries, she'll have some."

"Good to know."

"She not only runs the Gift Shop, she makes native clothing and slippers. And excellent beadwork," Tessa said. "She's a really nice lady, so don't be afraid to ask her for help."

"Thanks. And that man with her?"

"That's Jason Knight. He runs the Thomas Lounge and he's the chief bartender there."

They scooted past Nellie and Jason, unnoticed, and into the Coffee Shop.

The staff ate in the Alberta Rose Coffee Shop which was a large airy room with a tall ceiling, a hardwood floor, and clusters of small wooden tables and chairs. Less formal than the Foothills Dining Room, the Coffee Shop was still impressive. Huge framed maps hung on the dark mahogany woodwork. Philodendrons in wooden boxes decorated some of the nooks. Place settings sparkled with crystal goblets and silver flatware.

Tessa chose a table next to the door that led to the courtyard. She sat facing the room and let Mariah look out the lead-paned windows and the view.

Wearing the typical uniform of emerald green shirt and black pants, a server delivered their soup and sandwiches and coffee.

"This is Mariah," Tessa said. "She's a new maid. This is Greta."

Greta's brown hair was long and straight. Her bangs were sleek, and her dark brown eyes were bright and happy. She looked to be in her early twenties.

"Welcome to the Thurston Hotel," Greta said. "It'll be crazy busy this weekend, so don't let it get to you. By next Tuesday we'll be back to normal."

Greta left. Tessa took a sip of her soup, and then dropped the spoon in the bowl.

"Oh!" Her voice was almost a whisper.

"What?"

Tessa leaned forward and, in a low voice, she said, "Don't look now, but see those two old ladies?" She flicked a surreptitious look at the table across the aisle.

So did Mariah, and she recognized the two old ladies. Mrs. Jamieson and Mrs. Arbuckle were sitting down to lunch. They were as well-groomed and polished as they'd been last night.

Today, Mrs. Arbuckle wore a bright pink suit with matching earrings and lipstick. Her wavy white hair poofed around her head. Her eyebrows were carefully arched. And her intense blue eyes were highlighted by eyelashes thick with mascara. Probably in her late seventies, the spry little woman exuded friendliness and charm. She reminded Mariah of an old Betty White movie.

Mrs. Jamieson was about ten years younger, late sixties, and the more conservative of the two. Her white hair was smoother, her pink lipstick was more subdued and her whole manner was calmer. Even though she wore red, it was not a glaring color on her. It was simply her color.

Her eyes were blue as well. A deeper, darker blue than Mrs. Arbuckle.

"The one on the right is an owner of the hotel," Tessa said, speaking quietly. "Last year she was the manager. The one on the left lives here permanently, on the top floor."

Mariah felt like saying hello but she wasn't sure if the

staff, especially the maids, were supposed to acknowledge the upper class.

"They probably won't see us, but if they do, Mrs. Jamieson might complain that you're not wearing a name tag," Tessa said. "You should have one by tomorrow. I'll explain that you're new."

At any rate, the two matrons had not noticed them. They slanted toward each other across their table, heads close, as if scheming. They looked kind of cute.

"They spend a lot of time together, those two," Tessa said, in a hushed voice.

"Do they have husbands?"

"Both are widowed and both like to keep busy. They enjoy talking to the hotel guests. And matchmaking." Tessa giggled. "And interfering wherever they can."

Had one of them interfered last night? And turned this into a part-time position? Mariah sipped her cream of pumpkin soup, trying to remember last night's conversation. But the details were vague. Yesterday's long bus ride had tired her out so she must have misunderstood when she thought this was a full-time position.

Finally, after polishing off every crumb of her grilled cheese sandwich, only the coffee remained, a rich blend with a hint of hazelnut.

Maybe Tessa would have some suggestions about possible work. Might as well ask. "Do you know where I can get a second job?"

Tessa jerked, spilled some coffee, and her mouth dropped open. A deer caught in the headlights.

"A second job?" She sputtered. "What do you mean?"

A strange reaction. Maybe Tessa felt nervous sitting so close to the hotel management. "I mean," Mariah explained, "it turns out they only want me part time. I need to find other work."

"Oh, I see," Tessa answered, relief washing over her.

Then she frowned. "That's odd. Bailey asked me if I could do extra hours over the weekend," she said. "Because of all the extra guests with the Labor Day weekend."

"I know. I'll be full time over the weekend, but by Tuesday, I'm part time."

Tessa thought a moment. "The Clip and Curl," she said. "Dory could use some help, with sweeping, cleaning, making coffee. It's not a lot of money but it's something."

"Nearby?"

"Across the street. On your way back to the bus depot. Right around the corner from Sleek Chic."

"Good. I'll visit there on Tuesday. Sooner, if I get time."

"Not likely," Tessa said.

From the next table, Mariah heard the sound of chairs scraping on the hardwood. The two matrons had finished their lunch.

"We'd better get going," Tessa said. "There's still a lot to do."

Mariah finished with her serviette and prepared to get up, but suddenly Mrs. Jamieson stood at the end of the table, looking down at her.

Mrs. Arbuckle stood next to her, an impish expression on her face.

"Mind if we join you?" Mrs. Jamieson asked.

Chapter Five

"Oh! Sorry!" Tessa stumbled to her feet. "We didn't mean to take so long for lunch. We were just leaving."

"No rush," Mrs. Jamieson said. "Please sit down."

Flustered, Tessa sat, and Mrs. Arbuckle dragged two chairs across the aisle. Tessa and Mariah's table was only meant for two, so Mrs. Arbuckle tucked the chairs at the end of the table, blocking the aisle that led to the courtyard.

Not that the servers would ever complain.

Sitting beside Mariah, Mrs. Jamieson smiled and said, "I am Mrs. Jamieson." She paused, as if she were expecting a particular response. And then she added, "Mrs. Emily Thurston Jamieson."

She made it sound as if Mariah should recognize the name. Maybe the name had been in the news lately? Maybe Mariah should have read about it?

But she hadn't. So, although she'd never heard of Mrs. Jamieson before today, she said, "Yes, I know."

"You know?"

"Your niece Bailey mentioned your name this morning."

Mrs. Jamieson's lips curved down in a disappointed expression. "You know Bailey?"

"Bailey had me fill out hiring forms."

"Yes, of course she did," Mrs. Jamieson said. And then, as if in an effort to change the subject, "How is your day going?"

"It's going great. Tessa is an excellent teacher."

"We've finished all of our regular rooms," Tessa said, twisting her hands together. "We've just got the honeymoon suite left."

"The honeymoon suite!" Mrs. Arbuckle clasped her hands and her face lit up. "Oh that's charming!"

"The couple will arrive at five o'clock," Tessa said, checking her watch.

"I see." Mrs. Jamieson nodded. "So you're going up there now?"

"Yes. The heavy cleaning was finished yesterday. Now we're setting up the room."

"That sounds like fun." Mrs. Jamieson turned to Mariah. "Can we watch?"

Mariah shrugged. "Sure." And then she noticed that Tessa had that deer in the headlights look again.

"We have to get the cart," Tessa said. "You can meet us on the fourth floor. Room 47."

Two minutes later, in the service elevator, Tessa was hyperventilating. "Why is she coming to watch me work?"

"Not you," Mariah said. "Me."

"You? But why?"

"I told her I didn't have any experience. She probably wants to make sure I don't mess up the honeymoon suite."

Frowning, Tessa watched the numbers rise on the elevator. "Mrs. Jamieson hired you?"

"Yes, last night."

"Roberta didn't tell me that." Tessa let go of a pent-up breath. "I thought she was upset with my work. I've been tired lately, but—"

"You're doing a great job. They've been short-staffed. It makes sense you'd be tired."

And as easy as that, Tessa relaxed. "I'm fine now," she said. "And, you'll like this. It's actually fun doing the honeymoon suite."

The elevator dinged open on the fourth floor and they pushed the cart out. "They did a deep clean yesterday. The carpet and furniture have been shampooed. The mattress has been flipped. And the bathroom is already sanitized."

"What's left?"

"The special touches."

. . . . .

At the top of the Plain of Six Glaciers Trail, Teague had watched his tourists pile into the Tea House.

Some could have gone on, but most were tired.

With the weather cooperating, they'd had perfect views. They'd seen wildlife too. Today it was mostly marmots, chipmunks, squirrels, pikas, and off in the distance, one grizzly. At that point, Hazel Anderson had asked Shredder for her camera and he'd patiently retrieved it from his backpack.

She'd asked him for her camera again at the Tea House. After taking some photos of the view and the Tea House, she'd given it back to him and he'd returned it to his pack. He also carried the woman's binoculars. He'd carried both almost from the trailhead.

Now, filled with apple pie, biscuits and lemonade the group headed downhill for the return trip. As usual, downhill was more difficult for some.

"My knees are killing me," Hazel said.

Without any discussion, Shredder set his pack down, pulled out a pair of telescoping trekking poles, and adjusted them for Hazel's height.

"Use them like this," he said, demonstrating.

She caught on quickly and continued down the trail.

Of course, this meant Shredder had to carry her useless walking stick, but the kid didn't complain. Using a small bungee, he attached the walking stick to his pack. Then one of the other tourists, Quincy, came alongside Shredder. About the same age as Shredder, Quincy wore a short stylish haircut and designer hiking clothes.

"Where are the six glaciers?" he asked. "I could only see three."

"You have to walk further to see all six. That's a hike for another day."

A few paces later, Quincy had another question. "Who built the Tea House?"

"The Canadian Pacific Railway," Shredder said. "Their Swiss guides built the original in 1924 as a rest stop for mountain climbers."

The trail turned and Quincy pulled alongside Shredder again. "I want to video an avalanche. When is the next one happening?"

Shredder slowed, slightly, but kept walking. "Avalanches are a normal occurrence up here but we can't predict when they'll happen."

And then a few minutes later, "What's the name of that mountain?"

"That's Fairmont," Shredder answered.

After that Teague couldn't hear the conversation. He pulled back and waited for an older couple, checking that all was well.

· · · · ·

As Mariah and Tessa tightened the white linen sheets, the two matrons arrived.

Mrs. Arbuckle swept into the room, turning in circles, taking in the ambiance. "I have always loved this room. It's not as big as the honeymoon suite on my floor, but this one is more intimate."

Mrs. Jamieson slowly stepped into the room, waited at the entrance and appeared unaffected by the room's mood.

After a moment's consideration, she said, "I'm not sure I like the pink."

The room's bright pink walls reminded Mariah of the antacid liquid, Pepto-Bismol. Not only the color but the sensation she felt in her stomach.

"But the pink is so pretty," Mrs. Arbuckle argued. "Brides love pink."

"There are grooms to think of as well," Mrs. Jamieson said, flatly. "As far as I know, grooms do not love pink."

Mrs. Arbuckle would not be discouraged. "Oh well. A happy bride means a happy groom."

Mrs. Jamieson inspected the bed. "At least, we've switched from the pink linen."

Standing back, Mariah watched the interchange as she peeled the cellophane from a heart-shaped box of chocolates. At the same time, Tessa spread a large white bath towel on the end of the bed.

"Oh, no." Mrs. Jamieson put her hand to her heart. "We're still doing the swans?"

About to roll the towel, Tessa hesitated.

"Go ahead, Tessa. Do your swans." Mrs. Jamieson turned her back on Tessa, walked to the windows and pulled back the sheers to look out at the view.

Using two large white towels, Tessa rolled and folded and fanned, and finally created a large elaborate swan. She repeated the process with two more towels, and made a matching swan. Sitting at the foot of the bed, the swan heads touched, forming a heart. Then, using a purple orchid, Tessa provided the finishing touch by clamping the beaks together. Mariah found the whole production as nauseating as the pink walls.

Of course, it was a reaction to her own doomed wedding. Her own attempt at a fairy tale. Not that she ever would have done the swans.

But now she knew that fairy tales were not reality.

Princes did not exist. And, even if she ever met that Teague fellow again, she was not in the market for another disappointing prince.

"It's lovely," Mrs. Arbuckle crooned.

"It's cheesy," Mrs. Jamieson said. "And Tessa, I am not criticizing your work. Your work is excellent. I just don't like swans."

"I'm guessing now," Mrs. Arbuckle said. "But I take it you didn't have swans on your wedding night?"

Mrs. Jamieson looked across the room, at nothing in particular. "I didn't have a huge wedding," she said.

"Why not?" Mrs. Arbuckle asked as she studied the open box of chocolates, leaning in to sniff them. "Oh yes, you had to get married."

"Maddie!"

"It's nothing to be—"

"I don't want to talk about it. And do not eat any of those chocolates!"

Had to get married? That would mean she was pregnant before the wedding. And that would have constituted a scandal back in the day. But, no matter, Mrs. Jamieson seemed to have done well with her life.

Briefly, Mariah wondered if the child in question had ever felt unwanted.

While Tessa fussed with the swan feathers, Mariah placed large pink pillar candles on sturdy crystal saucers. A half dozen candles—that smelled like artificial strawberries.

"They all go on the bureau, in front of the mirror," Tessa said, tweaking one last fold on her swan.

Mariah lined up the candles. At least they would be out of reach of any flailing that might happen on the bed. And, she noticed, the room was set up with a smoke detector.

"Can you open the box from the florist?"

"I'll help," Mrs. Arbuckle said. And she did, pulling back the film around three arrangements of white roses mixed with pink daisies.

"One on either end of the bureau. One on the vanity in the bathroom," Tessa instructed.

Mrs. Arbuckle took care of the bureau flowers and Mariah carried the remaining arrangement into the bathroom. When she returned, Mrs. Arbuckle and Mrs. Jamieson stood near the windows, heads bent together, probably discussing Mrs. Jamieson's wedding night, or lack of.

"Bathrobes," Tessa said.

This task involved carefully folding the hotel's brilliant white bathrobes so the green TH monogram displayed to the best advantage. Then the robes were arranged by slightly overlapping them near the head of the bed, as if one robe cuddled the other.

Did honeymooners really need this much prompting?

"Now we sprinkle it all with rose petals," Tessa said. "Like this."

Rose petals. On white sheets. Didn't anyone consider the potential for stains? The laundry people must use lots of bleach after these occasions.

After she finished scattering rose petals over the whole bed, Tessa handed a box of supplies to Mariah. "You set out the votive candles in the bathroom," Tessa said. "The orchid goes on top of the towels. Put them beside the tub. I'll get the champagne flutes."

As Mariah carried the box and the orchid to the bathroom, she heard Mrs. Jamieson following her.

"I will assist," Mrs. Jamieson said.

· · · · ·

Teague stood beside the van in the parking lot at Lake Louise, waiting for the last few stragglers. Three were buying postcards. Four more were in the bathrooms. Two of them were getting their pictures taken with the bagpiper.

Tonight, he would find Mariah Patrick, and somehow, he would casually ask her to dinner in the Foothills Dining Room.

No, the dining room would be too formal. She wouldn't agree to a date. He had to make it look like it wasn't a date. Maybe he could get Bailey to invite her to the Thomas Lounge, and then he could just happen to bump into her. That might work.

Shredder finished loading the day packs. "Don't ask me to go hiking tomorrow," he said. "I can't stand it."

"You did a great job with Hazel Anderson."

"Yeah." He shrugged. "She did fine for a first-time hiker."

"So what's the problem?"

"The gorbies. I can't stand the gorbies."

"Quincy?"

"Yeah," Shredder said. "He's some kind of financial whiz kid at an oil company. Has to know everything."

"And that's tiring."

"He was asking me questions about Mount Fairmont."

"And?"

"He wanted to know how much the mountain weighed."

Seriously? "What did you say?"

Shredder grinned. "I said, with or without the trees?"

. . . . .

Mariah wondered, again, why Mrs. Jamieson was watching her so closely. Although Mariah had never been a maid, she felt like she was getting it right. Hopefully, she would measure up. She needed this job.

The large and elegant bathroom radiated calm, especially after the hot pink, rose-littered bedroom. In here, white fixtures, gray tile floor, and light gray walls combined to make a quiet retreat. Moss green tile formed a wide surround for the corner whirlpool tub. And there was no pink in sight, except for the white rose and pink daisy bouquet on the spacious gray marble countertop.

Mariah moved the stack of fluffy white towels from the countertop to the tub surround and set the purple orchid on top of the stack.

Mrs. Jamieson sat on the other end of the tub and surveyed the room. "This is perfect," she said. "An excellent renovation. Much classier than that pink they had before."

While the old woman commented, Mariah worked at the countertop, setting the votive candles into their crystal holders.

"Add the bubbling bath salts before you leave," Mrs. Jamieson said. "After they have their honeymoon dinner in the Foothills Dining Room, you will come up and run the tub. Make it the perfect temperature. The groom wants to lower his bride into the water. Once the bubbles are frothy, sprinkle the rose petals over top. Then light the candles and turn out the lights."

"Bubbles, rose petals, candles, no lights. Got it," Mariah said, smiling. The whole production seemed over the top. She turned and noticed Mrs. Jamieson was smiling too.

"Yes, really," Mrs. Jamieson said. "I know it's ridiculous but it's what they asked for."

Mariah felt a camaraderie with her boss. At least they had the same opinion of pink walls and tub preparation.

"What brings you to Harmony?" Mrs. Jamieson asked.

Long story, Mariah thought, as she lowered a candle into its holder. And not one she fully wanted to tell. "I needed to start over."

"After the wildfires."

"Yes, but it was time to leave anyway." She set the last

candle in place. "Do you like lavender?"

"Not particularly. Why?"

Mariah opened the jar of *Spirit Song Lavender Bubbling Bath Salts* and tested the scent. "It doesn't seem like a good choice for a bridal suite."

"It's supposed to be calming and soothing."

"It smells like an old person." *Whoops.* She was talking to an old person.

"Yes, I agree," Mrs. Jamieson said, as if they were discussing paint chips. "And yes, I know I'm an old person."

"Sorry. I didn't mean—"

"You're right," Mrs. Jamieson said, with a confident tone, one that suggested she was assessing a focus group's appraisal. "We should come up with a different scent. Do you have any suggestions?"

Mariah poured the appropriate dose of bath salts into the tub. "Something fresh. And new. Something spicy." She recapped the bottle. "Maybe orange blossom."

"Good." Mrs. Jamieson nodded. "I'll pass that along to Ben."

"Ben?"

Mrs. Jamieson raised her eyebrows. "Don't tell me you don't know him."

"I haven't had time to meet everyone."

For some reason, Mrs. Jamieson's look suggested suspicion. Almost as if she thought Mariah had ulterior motives for being here. *Odd.*

"Ben Thurston," Mrs. Jamieson said. She sat up perfectly straight, looking regal from her perch on the tub surround. "He's the hotel manager."

"Bailey's brother?"

"Yes," she said, with her chin held high. "So you *do* know him."

"No, I haven't met him yet. But this morning Bailey

mentioned her brother managed the hotel."

The old woman stared at her like she was trying to see inside her. And then she suddenly looked pale, and wan.

"You used to be the manager," Mariah said.

Mrs. Jamieson heaved a long sigh. "Until last August."

"And then?"

"I had a heart attack."

Mariah felt a rush of sympathy for the old woman. It must have been difficult for her to give up her job. No wonder she still wanted to be active in the hotel's management. "How are you feeling now?"

"Tired," she said. "A lot."

"What meds are you on?"

Perking up slightly, she said, "I'm on a calcium channel blocker if that means anything to you."

"It does. And I'm guessing you're too active to be on a beta blocker. Have you tried an ACE inhibitor?"

"I—I don't know. There was another drug, but I had side effects."

"Tell your doctor the medication is making you tired and you want to try something different. It takes a few tries to find the best drug."

Mrs. Jamieson squinted at her. "Are you on blood pressure medication?"

"No."

"Is your mother on heart medication?"

Mariah felt her jaw drop. *Why all these questions?* "No."

"Then how do you know about blood pressure medications?"

How indeed. "Jill-of-all-trades," Mariah said, and she was not saying more.

She expected Mrs. Jamieson to quiz her further, but the old woman switched topics.

"Why did you choose Harmony?"

Mariah wondered that herself. "I have no idea.

Something about the place kept calling to me and I made one of those spur of the moment decisions."

"Were you out of work?"

"No. I had work on one of the cleanup crews. Manual labor, shoveling, sweeping, clearing away rubble."

"Sounds like hard work."

"It was. But I needed the money to pay off some debts. And now here I am."

"Interesting," Mrs. Jamieson said, looking down at the bath salts scattered in the bottom of the tub. "Have you ever been married?"

"Almost," Mariah answered, without thinking. She had not wanted to volunteer that information.

"Almost?"

"It's a sore spot. I'd rather not talk about it."

It was also why she was having nothing to do with Teague, no matter how many meals he offered her. She didn't need or want a man in her life.

"Is that part of the reason you left Fort McMurray?"

"Yes, it is. It's a very big part of why I left."

"Who was he?"

Enough. "Mrs. Jamieson, you can watch me work, but I won't discuss my love life. Or lack of."

Rather than be offended by Mariah's answer, Mrs. Jamieson appeared pleased. She nodded quickly and stood up, spryly. Almost as if she were satisfied with the non-answer.

"Of course. I didn't mean to pry," she said, with a tone of apology. "Everything looks fine here. Let's check the rest of the room."

By this time, Tessa had dealt with the coffee table. It now held a bouquet of long-stemmed red roses, a wicker fruit basket and a champagne holder.

"Gill will bring up the ice and champagne as soon as the couple arrives," Tessa said. She checked her watch.

"And that will be in about an hour. It's four o'clock now."

"So we're done?" Mrs. Arbuckle asked. "That was fun."

"One more thing." Tessa crossed the room to the CD player. She touched a button, the tray slid open and she checked the five discs inside. Then she tapped a button and the tray slid closed.

"What kind of music do young people play on their wedding night?" Mrs. Arbuckle asked.

"Some couples bring their own music," Tessa told them, "but we have jazz ready to go."

"I like jazz," Mrs. Arbuckle said. As she said it, the lights flickered, went out for about three seconds, and then came back on.

"Do we have a wiring issue?" Mrs. Jamieson looked concerned. "Or is that from outside?"

"It's from outside," Mrs. Arbuckle said. "Walter never liked jazz."

Walter? Who was Walter? And what did he have to do with the lights?

Mariah glanced at Tessa to see if she understood. Tessa closed her eyes and shook her head no. And then they heard the commotion in the hallway.

"Bill! Bill! Help me! Please!"

Chapter Six

The world's slowest elevator stopped at the fourth floor. Teague and Shredder, each with an arm around Hazel Anderson, carried her out. Behind them, Gill stumbled and dropped Hazel's walking stick in front of Shredder. Shredder tripped, fell, and took Hazel with him. They landed in a heap on the floor.

"Bill! Bill! Help me! Please!"

Poor Hazel. Her chin-length, gray-blonde hair hung in straggles around her weary face. She'd survived her first hike, but after sitting in the van for the trip back to Harmony, her muscles had seized up, making her stiff and sore. And now this.

"Whoops," Gill said. "Sorry." He picked up the walking stick, and Hazel's day pack, and her hat.

Shredder popped to his feet. "I'm fine, Boss," he said. "Don't worry about me."

Teague bent to help Hazel, but stopped. Because in the next instant, the waif rounded the corner from the hallway to the elevators.

She knelt beside Hazel and grasped the woman's wrist. And it looked as if she was . . . checking her pulse? After a few seconds, she stared into Hazel's eyes.

Checking pupil reaction?

No, he was imagining things. Then Tessa arrived.

"I'm fine," Hazel said. "A little worse for wear, but I'm fine."

Mariah sent him a questioning glance.

"She tripped."

Her mouth dropped open but no words came out.

"Hiking," he said.

Mariah blinked. "Did she want to go hiking?"

"Of course she did. Didn't you, Hazel?"

"Yes, I did. It was my first time."

Teague looked back at Mariah and couldn't resist the challenge. "*She* likes trying new things," he said.

"Your husband is down in the Peaks Bar." Gill juggled the walking stick and the day pack and the Aussie hat. "Do you want me to get him?"

"No." Hazel pushed herself up to a sitting position. "He didn't think I should go hiking. He didn't think I was fit enough." She grimaced. "He may have been right."

"She's stiff and sore," Teague said, speaking to Mariah, "but otherwise she's okay." He crouched down beside Hazel. "You did great for your first hike. And once you have a long hot shower, you'll feel better."

Mariah sat back on her heels, studying Hazel. "Do you have ibuprofen with you?"

"What's that?"

"Advil," Teague said.

"Oh," Hazel answered. "No, I don't."

He should probably have it available for first-time hikers. But, never mind Advil, he could hear more people approaching. Expecting a scene, he saw Mrs. Jamieson and Mrs. Arbuckle round the corner from the hallway.

Great. They were going to make a fuss about one of his clients falling down. But . . . what were those two doing on the fourth floor? Mrs. Arbuckle lived on the sixth floor, not the fourth.

"What happened?" Mrs. Jamieson asked.

And almost at the same time, Mrs. Arbuckle asked, "Are you all right?"

"She's fine, muscle soreness. That's all," Teague told them. He noticed Shredder moving off to the side.

"Gill?" Mariah caught the bellhop's attention. "Put those things down. Go to the gift shop. See if they have Advil or some kind of ibuprofen and bring it here for Mrs.—" Mariah returned her attention to Hazel.

"Mrs. Anderson," Hazel said. "But please call me Hazel."

"Okay, Hazel. What room are you in?"

"Number 48."

Mariah looked up at Gill, raised her eyebrows. Gill set Hazel's things on the floor and headed for the stairs. At the top step, he stumbled, recovered and then continued down.

"Are you sure you're all right?" Mrs. Jamieson asked. "Why are you sitting on the floor?"

"I tripped," Hazel said. "But I'm fine. Really, I am."

"Tessa?" Mariah still knelt on the floor. "Can you bring Hazel's things to her room."

Tessa collected the items that Gill had dropped. The walking stick, the day pack and Hazel's hat.

Meanwhile, Shredder hung back, standing near the elevator. Finally, Mrs. Jamieson noticed him.

"Who are you?" she asked.

"Shredder McGee," he said with a quirk of a smile.

"Shredder?" Mrs. Jamieson frowned. "What kind of a name is that?"

"It's my name," Shredder said. A full smile. "Who are you?"

Mrs. Jamieson drew herself up tall. "I am Mrs. Emily— oh, what's the use." She pushed the elevator button. "Let's go, Maddie," she said. "Mariah has everything under control." The elevator, still on the fourth floor, dinged open and the two old ladies left.

Teague got to his feet. "Go back to the store," he told Shredder. "See if Monroe needs any help."

"Sure thing, Boss." Shredder headed to the stairs and in two seconds he was gone.

Mariah got to her feet.

Teague looked right at her, right into those pretty blue eyes. "Room 48?"

She nodded. "It's at the end of the hall. On the left side."

Not far, since the bank of elevators was in the center of the building. He could help Hazel walk, but it would be a long shuffle for her. Plus, up here, there wouldn't be a bunch of hotel guests and staff watching. Hopefully.

He bent, gathered Hazel in his arms and lifted her.

"Oh my!"

He carried her down the hall. Mariah ran ahead, light and nimble on her feet. Tessa followed behind him. By the time they reached Hazel's suite, Mariah had unlocked the door with her maid keycard and was holding it open for him. He set Hazel in one of the room's armchairs.

"Thank you so much," Hazel said. "I could not have walked another step."

Tessa tossed Hazel's day pack and hat on the bed, and propped her walking stick in a corner. Mariah came out of the bathroom with a glass of water and handed it to Hazel. And Gill breezed into the room.

"I've got the Advil," he announced, giving the bottle to Mariah.

She read the label, shook out two tablets and put them in Hazel's hand. "I'll run the tub for you," she said.

Hazel downed the pills. "I don't want to be a bother."

"It's no problem," Mariah told her.

No problem? To him, she looked tired, and she probably was, since she'd worked all day. She needed a break. And from what he knew of her so far, she'd resist taking one. But he had an idea. "You'll join the rest of us in the Thomas Lounge?" he asked Hazel.

Hazel didn't seem to remember. "The Thomas Lounge?"

"The hiking group is meeting in the Thomas Lounge tonight," Teague reminded her. "To celebrate trying new things."

"Oh," she said, considering it, unenthusiastically.

"You'll be there, right, Hazel?"

"I don't know. I'm pretty tired."

"Have that hot shower first." Or maybe the bath would be more effective. He looked at Mariah. "Or that hot bath." Mariah nodded and he turned back to Hazel. "After that, you can decide, okay?"

"Okay, I'll try to be there."

"Mariah will come too," he said. "She likes to try new things."

The waif leveled a look at him. But he thought she was trying not to smile.

"Tessa? You should come too." Tessa would have a better chance of talking Mariah into the idea.

"I'm sorry," Tessa said. "I can't. I've got something tonight. But you should go, Mariah. You'll meet some of the other staff."

"Need anything else?" Gill asked, standing at the door.

"We're fine," Mariah said. "Now go away. Hazel is going to have a nice long soak in the tub."

"Oh! Gill!" Tessa stopped him. "The room is ready for the honeymoon couple. They'll need ice and the champagne right after they arrive." She checked her watch. "Should be in about forty-five minutes."

"No, they'll be late," Gill said. "They phoned. They'll be arriving closer to seven. They're driving from somewhere far away."

· · · · ·

At eight o'clock, Teague opened the twin white-framed glass doors and walked into the Thomas Lounge—a large impressive room with an unexpected cozy feel.

The décor consisted of cream-colored walls, tall mahogany accents, big art, wall sconce lighting and an elaborate red rug with a pattern of gold twining through it. That was the impressive part. That, and Jason's expansive bar on the right side of the room.

The chairs were the cozy part. The chairs and the different sized tables. Some round tables and some square and some rectangular ones. Large and small, they clustered throughout the room.

Each table had a different set of armchairs. All upholstered. Some with the arms upholstered. Some with wooden arms. Different fabrics—stripes, tapestry and plain. An eclectic and friendly combination.

Tonight, with the beginning of the long weekend, the room bubbled with high level conversations and lots of laughing. Somewhere in the background, he could faintly hear the usual, soothing and melodic instrumental music.

Shredder had claimed a long table at the back for the hiking group. Most of the hikers were there and, surprisingly, so was Hazel Anderson.

Teague recognized some of the waiters and noticed that new ones circulated, probably here specifically for the long weekend. Jason worked the bar and he also had extra help.

Mandy Brighton sat in a corner with one of her staff. Next to her table were Jim Barnes and Nick Danyluck. They saw him, waved, and went back to their conversation. Mackenzie Berg, at the end of the bar, chatted with her grandfather.

He recognized a few others. But there was no sign of the waif.

Not wanting to join the hikers yet, he found a seat at the bar. Jason delivered a Rickard's Red as soon as Teague sat down.

"How's it going?" Jason opened the beer.

"Good," Teague answered. "Have you seen the new maid?"

A slight pause from Jason. "Mariah?"

"Yes."

"About five foot seven? Long reddish brown hair? Blue eyes? Pleasant expression?"

"Yes."

"No, I haven't seen her," Jason said. "I haven't even met her."

Something was up. "Then how come you know what she looks like?"

"Because everybody's looking for Mariah."

Jason peered across the room. "That woman with the gray and blonde hair, at the table with all the hikers," he said. "That's Hazel Anderson, Brock's mother."

"I know. I took her hiking today."

"She went hiking? She looks too old. Where'd you go?"

"She's early sixties. Tops. And she did fine. We went to the Plain of Six Glaciers."

Jason lifted his eyebrows. "Good for her," he said. "That's her husband with her. Bill Anderson. They want to buy dinner for Mariah."

Jason leaned across the bar, keeping his voice low, "And over there." He angled his head toward where Mrs. Jamieson and Mrs. Arbuckle sat at a small table. "Mrs. Jamieson. She wants to buy dinner for Mariah too."

That didn't make sense. "Why?"

"How should I know? Maybe this Mariah maid messed up. Maybe Mrs. Jamieson is going to complain," Jason said. "Maybe she's softening the blow by feeding her first."

How badly could Mariah mess up on her first day?

"Who else is looking for her?"

"Bailey."

"Bailey?"

"No doubt, work-related."

"Any idea where she is?"

"Mariah or Bailey?"

"Mariah."

"The Clip and Curl," Jason said. "Turns out Mariah's job is part time and she needs money."

"She told you that?"

"Tessa told me that. And Tessa suggested the Clip and Curl. Dory needs someone to sweep the floor."

"Is Mariah there now?"

"Probably."

Someone sat down next to him. Turning, he saw Bailey Thurston.

"Hi," she said. And then, to Jason, "I'll get a glass of red wine. The house is fine."

Teague waited until she had her wine, then he started. "You have a new hire?"

"Don't tell me. You're looking for Mariah Patrick too?"

"I heard *you* were looking for her," Teague said.

"I need to send her upstairs for a job. Soon." Bailey took a sip of the wine. "And my aunt is looking for her."

"Because?"

"No idea." Bailey twisted her wine glass and watched the liquid wave. "Aunt Emily hired her last night. I'm not sure why."

He wasn't sure why either. Could have been because Roberta had been so abrupt. Could have been because Mrs. Jamieson felt sorry for the waif. But, regardless, Mariah didn't seem like a maid.

"Not maid material?"

"She's doing the job," Bailey said, still swirling her wine. "No complaints from Tessa. I get the impression—"

Bailey must have realized this was none of his business. And, strictly speaking, it wasn't. "You owe me," he said.

She considered him a moment. "You like her."

"I might."

Bailey smiled, and he knew that she knew exactly how much he liked Mariah Patrick.

"So? What's her story?"

A short beat, a moment to consider. "She needs the money," Bailey said, with a serious voice. "So she'll take anything."

"Background?"

"Don't know much. She's taking business courses online. Wants to go to university when she gets the money."

Interesting. "Family?"

"None that I know of. She's from Fort Mac, so I expect she lost everything there last May."

That might explain the need for money. The fire had affected a lot of people.

"When did you meet her?" Bailey asked.

"At the bus station yesterday."

"I see."

He didn't see. And he had no idea why Mariah didn't want anything to do with him.

"Don't come on too strong," Bailey told him. "I get the sense she's been unlucky in love."

Unlucky? Some jerk had hurt her? What kind of idiot would do that?

"Approach her slowly," Bailey said. "Like approaching a squirrel."

"A squirrel?"

"Best to let her come to you."

Bailey might have a point. "Thanks."

They sipped their drinks, he glanced at the door a few times, checked his watch. A quarter past eight.

"How did your hike go with Mrs. Anderson?" Bailey asked.

"Hazel?"

"You're calling the lawyer's wife Hazel?"

"She told me to," Teague said, knowing how Bailey followed protocol. "Important guest?"

"They're all important," Bailey said. "But Mrs. Anderson is the mother of the groom. You know that." Bailey studied her wine. "The bride's parents are showing up tomorrow night." She closed her eyes briefly, a little grimace. "Should be interesting."

Bailey would be worried about Lilith Hamilton, the bride's mother, and . . . the mayor's wife. "You mean, Mrs. Mayor Ed Hamilton."

"The same." Bailey let go of a long sigh.

Lilith Hamilton didn't have a lot of people skills, but she did get things done. "It's because of her you renovated the ballroom." Teague had heard about that. About how the mother of the bride would not agree to the Thurston Hotel as the venue for the wedding, not unless they did the renovations.

"No," Bailey said, firmly. "Lilith was the catalyst, but it needed to be done."

At that moment, Hazel Anderson sat down on the other side of Bailey.

"You're looking much better," Teague said.

"I feel wonderful. Thank you." She touched Bailey's shoulder.

"Bailey, I wanted to thank you for the nurse."

"The . . . nurse?"

"She got me some Advil for the pain," Hazel said. "She gave me a massage and that whirlpool was heavenly. Especially with the lavender."

Bailey squinted. "Are you in a whirlpool room?"

"No, but there's one across the hall. The nurse said it's for a honeymoon couple but they're arriving late, so she insisted I make use of the tub."

Bailey kept listening and nodding, with her mouth partly open.

"After she finished with me, she set up the tub again. And then she put a tensor bandage on my ankle. Now I feel excellent." She leaned around Bailey to look at him. "The hike was invigorating. I'm so glad I went."

"And the nurse's name?" Bailey asked.

"Mariah."

"She's not a nurse," Bailey said, shaking her head. "She's a maid."

Hazel glowed. "Then your hotel has the best maids I've ever met. And Teague?" She got his attention again. "I'm impressed with your guide Shredder. Those trekking poles he gave me worked so much better than my walking stick. And he carried all my stuff."

"I'm glad he could help you."

"Does your store sell those trekking poles?"

"Yes, we do."

"Then I'll be by tomorrow to purchase my own. Are you joining our table?"

"I will," Teague said. "In a few minutes."

Hazel walked back to Shredder's table, with not a trace of a limp.

"I can't believe she did that." Bailey spread her hands on the bar and stared at them.

"She's actually a strong hiker," Teague said.

"Not her. Mariah. What if the honeymooners had shown up and their room was in use?"

Not the worst thing in the world. But, he supposed, things like that were important to the hotel's image. "Are they here yet?"

"Yes." Bailey seemed impatient. "They're in the Foothills Dining Room and as soon as they order dessert, I need Mariah to go up there and run their tub."

"They can't run their own tub?"

Bailey pressed her hand on her forehead and squeezed her temples.

Then Gill arrived, still in uniform, so obviously still on duty. "They've ordered dessert," he told Bailey.

She checked her watch, and glanced at the door. "Finally."

Teague turned in the direction Bailey was looking. The entrance to the lounge, where Mariah stood in front of the twin doors.

Her hair was wet and pulled back in a ponytail. She wore a pair of faded jeans, a light green tunic top, and she looked like she'd seen a ghost. At least, her creamy white skin was more pale than usual. Standing still, she pressed the flat of her hand over her chest, like she was pushing something against her heart.

"I'll send her upstairs." Bailey slipped off her chair and marched toward the entrance.

From his spot at the bar, Teague watched as Bailey spoke quickly. But, Mariah didn't seem to be listening. Her gaze was on the carpet at her feet, and she kept her hand pressed over her heart.

Bailey touched Mariah's shoulder, gave her a little shake.

That seemed to snap her out of whatever it was. She straightened her shoulders, lifted her chin, and left the lounge.

Unable to stop himself, he headed for the door. When he got there, Bailey glared at him. "You're following her?"

"She's going to the fourth floor?"

"Yes, but—"

He kept going, and from behind him, he heard Bailey say, with a touch of resignation, "You're coming on too strong."

He didn't care. He needed to know what was happening that had made her look so . . . so fragile and hurt.

He waited in the lobby, around the corner from the elevator bay, until he heard the ding of the elevator door, heard it open, and close. Then he ran up the stairs to the fourth floor and waited on the lower landing, by the turn in the stairs, in time to hear the elevator arrive. Not much of a race considering how slow that thing was.

She left the elevator bay, and stomped down the hall, in the same direction as Hazel's suite.

Feeling like a spy and feeling somewhat ridiculous, he peeked around the corner, and watched her open a door at the end of the hall, presumably the honeymoon suite. It was on the opposite side of the hall from Hazel Anderson's suite and a few feet further down.

Now what?

If he waited for her to finish filling the tub, she'd probably rush back to the staff room and avoid him. And even if she went to the Thomas Lounge, she'd avoid him there too.

Unable to stop himself, he skulked down the hall. When he reached the door, he raised his hand to knock, but at the last second he stopped himself.

This was not a good idea.

Rubbing both hands over his head, he backed across the hall expecting to lean against the wall. But he almost lost his balance. Behind him was the supply room door, and it had been left ajar.

And then, almost simultaneously, two things happened. From down the hall, he heard the elevator doors ding open, and he heard low laughter. A second later, the latch on the honeymoon suite clicked. About to open.

Panicked, he slipped into the supply closet, and lightly closed the door. Taking his hands from the latch, he breathed a sigh of relief as he backed into the dark little room.

In the next moment, the door yanked open. Mariah raced inside, spun around and pulled the door closed.

Chapter Seven

She listened, with her ear pressed against the door, and she heard them arrive at their suite, laughing.

"Everything is ready, darling. You're going to love this."

A blanket of betrayal washed over her. She should have suspected, but she hadn't. She'd been so in love, so trusting, so stupid.

Disgusted with herself, she took her ear away from the door and stepped back, colliding with a hard warm body.

Shock rippled through her. Instinctively she started to scream. But all she got out was a squeak before a hand clamped over her mouth and a strong arm banded around her waist, pulling her back against that hard body.

She struggled, and the arm tightened.

"Calm down," someone whispered in her ear. "It's me."

She went still. *Me?* She searched, trying to recognize the voice, the whisper.

"It's me," the voice whispered again. "Teague. If you're hiding for some reason—and I think you are—you'd better be quiet."

When she heard his name, her heart tumbled and fell, and she slumped against him. Chasing right after that sensation was a mass of confusion. *Did this guy ever give up? How dare he follow her!* She struggled again.

And again, he tightened his hold on her. "No," he whispered.

Outside the supply closet door was the sound of noisy laughter and insipid giggling. The suite's door opened, the chunking sound of the lock engaging. The laughter retreated and the door swung shut with a loud click.

"You'll be quiet?" He took his hand from her mouth, but he kept his arm around her, kept her back pulled against his chest.

"Of course I will," she said, speaking out loud, but quietly. "Let go of me."

He didn't. Part of her was glad he kept hold of her, because her bravado was failing. When she'd come up to the honeymoon suite, her plan had seemed like a good idea. But not now. Now, a whole slew of doubts were sneaking between the cracks of her resolve.

She'd reacted instinctively, with rage, and she'd gone ahead with this poorly formed scheme. But, no matter, what was done, was done. If she lost her job over this, she'd find another. Anyway, she already had a second job at the Clip and Curl. But she'd have to find another place to live, and that—

"Are you going to tell me what you're up to?"

Back to her immediate problem. "No," she whispered.

"Do you know those people?"

She didn't want to answer. And she didn't want him touching her, and yet . . . she did. She didn't want him holding her, and somehow, she did.

She didn't want these contradicting emotions zooming around inside her. And for sure, she didn't want to be in this small space with Teague.

"I said, let go."

This time, he released her. And she immediately felt the loss of his touch. His support.

Support? What was she thinking? How could she even consider that he might support her? No one would support her. No one would help her. She was on her own.

Reaching in the dark, she felt for the door latch, opened it and leapt out of the small dark room. It took a moment for her eyes to adjust to the light of the hallway. And then she saw him. The old gentleman from the bus.

He still wore the same clothes, the navy blue sports jacket, the pale blue striped shirt with the button down collar. And maybe that wasn't odd. Maybe he hadn't packed a lot of things for his trip. Maybe he relied on the hotel's laundry, because that shirt looked crisp and fresh.

He leaned against the wall next to the door of the honeymoon suite, with his arms folded and a big smile on his face.

"What are you doing here?" she asked him.

He winked at her and his smile broadened.

"I was worried about you," Teague said, from behind her.

Then they heard the scream, coming from inside the honeymoon suite. A long, shrill, spine-chilling screech.

She could have stayed hidden in the closet. With Teague, so close. But that was the frying pan, and now she was in the fire. Surprisingly, she didn't care.

"Should we check?" Teague looked concerned.

Of course, he'd be concerned. Who wouldn't? But *he* looked especially concerned, like he was ready to break down that door and find out what was happening.

"Where's your keycard?" he asked. "Can you open the door?"

"Don't worry."

"*Don't worry?*"

"Wait for it," she said.

. . . . .

Teague stood next to Mariah, facing the door of the honeymoon suite. Down the hall, a woman poked her head out of her room. "Everything all right?" Another door opened and a man stepped into the hall. "What's all the ruckus?"

He had no idea, but Mariah did. She'd gone from looking scared to looking . . . vindicated? And, although he was clueless as to what was happening, he had to admit, it had been nice, holding her so close in the supply closet. He wouldn't mind doing that again.

His thoughts scattered with the sound of the latch clicking, and he braced, ready for anything.

The door jerked open and a frenzied-looking man stood there wearing a Thurston Hotel bathrobe. "You?" The man stared, eyes wide, completely focused on Mariah. "You!" he bellowed.

"Me." She smiled, and then she laughed. A laugh that started light and joyous, and then grew loud and wholehearted, until she was bent over holding her belly.

The man did not get the joke, whatever the joke was.

"You!" he screamed. "I should have known!" He raised his clenched fists and lurched toward her.

Teague slipped between them, and the man's hands landed on Teague's arms. "Don't even think about it," Teague said.

Distracted, the man noticed Teague, and flinched. But he snapped his attention back to Mariah.

Pointing his finger at her, he stormed on. "I don't know how you did it, but I should have known you'd do something like this."

From behind the man, a woman with dripping wet hair squeezed into the doorway. She also wore a Thurston Hotel bathrobe. Her eye makeup dripped onto her cheeks, and the rest of her dripped onto the carpet.

"Mariah?" She gaped, a smear of lipstick oozing onto her chin. "What are you doing here?"

"Hello, Olivia," Mariah said. Now the laughter was

punctuated with hiccups.

"She's a vindictive little witch," the man yelled. "I heard you'd left town but I had no idea you'd go to these lengths. No idea you could be so immature, so, so—Stop laughing! This is not funny!"

Gill came rushing down the hall. "Is everything all right? We got a call that someone screamed." He unclipped his two-way radio.

"Yes! Someone screamed! I lowered my wife into the tub and it was freezing cold and this woman is responsible and I want her removed from the hotel." The man paused for breath. "Now!"

Gill keyed the radio, and raised it to speak. "Roberta? You'd better send Bailey up here. Fourth floor. Honeymoon suite. Right away."

. . . . .

Teague stationed himself at the back of Bailey's office. Technically, he had no reason to be here, but he wasn't leaving. Not with the waif looking so upset.

Mrs. Arbuckle and Mrs. Jamieson also had no reason to be here, and yet the two old ladies sat in the guest chairs in front of Bailey's desk. Mrs. Arbuckle was on the left, closest to where he stood. Mrs. Jamieson sat in the middle. And, to the right of Mrs. Jamieson, Mariah sat on a folding chair.

More like, she huddled on the chair. With her elbows pulled in and her head down, she examined a loose thread on the hem of her tunic shirt.

Now that he thought about it, Mrs. Jamieson was probably here to do the firing, since she was the one who had hired Mariah last night. Mrs. Arbuckle would be along for the entertainment value and the chance to be in on the gossip.

The two old ladies leaned close together, muttering.

"I'm actually quite impressed with the performance," Mrs. Arbuckle said.

"Just like her mother," Mrs. Jamieson commented, happily. "Mind of her own, headstrong, determined, stubborn."

This firing session had probably interrupted their soap opera discussion so they continued it here.

The waif didn't seem to notice the old ladies, or him. She looked lost and alone, like she didn't have a friend in the world.

Finally, Bailey arrived. Tired and fuming, she swept into the room and headed around the desk. As she sank into her chair, Gill raced into the office.

"I've delivered a fresh bottle of champagne and a dozen roses and three boxes of Guy's best chocolates."

"And the bath?"

"Poppy is up there now. She's taking care of it. Fresh towels and flowers too."

"Good," Bailey said. "Is he happy?"

Bailey meant the noisy guest. The guy who couldn't take a joke.

"Not really," Gill answered.

"Is he quiet?"

"Yes."

"Stick around the desk. If he calls down for anything, give it to him."

Gill saluted her and scooted out of the office.

Bailey pressed her hands on the desk, closed her eyes and took a long slow breath. Then she opened her eyes and glared at Mariah. "Explain."

Looking fragile and determined at the same time, Mariah sat up straight on the hard chair. "His name is Colby Clifford," she said.

"I know his name."

Mariah swallowed. "His . . . *wife* . . . is Olivia Nealy."

"Go on."

Mariah sat ramrod straight, eyes ahead but not on Bailey, more like she was watching something unseen.

"She was almost my maid of honor," Mariah said in a small voice. "Last January."

Bailey opened her mouth, a slight pause. "And?"

"And *he* was almost my husband."

Silence for a long beat. "I see."

With a jolt, Teague saw too. No wonder Mariah wanted nothing to do with him. Well, maybe not him in particular. But it made sense she would be leery of relationships.

Mrs. Arbuckle gave a quick laugh. Mrs. Jamieson elbowed her.

Bailey nodded and studied the wood grain of her desk. Then she caught Mariah's attention. "Cold water *and* ice?"

"Yes."

"Where'd you get the ice?"

"The champagne bucket."

"That's—" Bailey thought about it. "Resourceful."

"Yes, it is," Mrs. Arbuckle commented. "And just remember, you can always get more ice from the machine by the elevators."

Mrs. Jamieson leveled a glance at her friend and Mrs. Arbuckle quieted.

Bailey pressed her lips together, thinking, and then she heaved out a long sigh. "This is unfortunate," she said, drumming the fingers of her right hand on the desk. "Is this why you wanted the job?"

Mariah's eyebrows shot up and she jerked her gaze to Bailey. "Absolutely not!"

"There, there," Mrs. Jamieson patted Mariah's knee. "No need to get all excited."

"I had—*no* idea they'd be here," Mariah stammered. "I had no idea they were getting married." She paused, took a long breath. "I had no idea they were engaged." The steam had gone out of her and she slumped in her chair. "I, basically, had no idea."

And he'd had no idea. No wonder Mariah was skittish. But was she still in love with that jerk?

The room was quiet. Even Mrs. Arbuckle was quiet. The two old ladies waited, perhaps hoping for a more entertaining story than the soap opera they'd been discussing.

"He called off the wedding," Mariah said, speaking to no one in particular. "On the morning of the wedding." She twisted her neck right and left, as if she were getting out kinks. "He sent Olivia with a note for me, saying he would not be there."

She frowned, probably thinking back through what had happened that day. Probably making sense of it now.

"I was supposed to send the guests home," she said. "But I didn't."

"No, you wouldn't," Mrs. Jamieson said.

Mariah ignored the interruption and kept talking. "I told them to go to the hall and enjoy the food. And the music. And the whole thing." She shrugged, in a defeated way. "Apparently, it was a great party."

No one spoke for a moment, and then Mrs. Jamieson did. "The hall, and the catering. Did he pay for that?"

"No," Mariah said. A heavy sigh. "And to be fair, it was my idea, to turn the reception into a party."

"He didn't pay for *any* of it?" Mrs. Jamieson asked again.

Mariah turned to Mrs. Jamieson. "I don't want to talk about it."

Bailey touched her teeth to her lower lip and sucked in some air. "Okay. What to do." She drummed her fingers again. "You haven't had dinner, have you?"

"No time."

"No time," Bailey repeated. "Right. Where did you go

after you and Tessa finished for the day?"

"The Clip and Curl. I got a second job for when I'm finished the day shift here."

Bailey held her hand out, palm up. "Because?"

"I need the money. I had a lot of debts in Fort Mac. The bill for the wedding was the biggest, but not the only one. And there was the fire. I lost a lot." Mariah played with the loose thread on her tunic again. "I'm out of debt now, but I need money for university. And to live."

"And for dinner," Teague said.

Bailey pursed her lips and gave him a small glance.

"Just saying," he answered, and then he decided to stay out of this. For the time being.

"Hazel Anderson wants to buy you dinner." Bailey said. "But—"

"Does she really want to be called by her first name?" Mrs. Jamieson asked. "Mrs. Anderson is Brock Anderson's mother, after all." Mrs. Jamieson wrinkled her forehead.

"She likes to be called Hazel," Bailey said.

"Humph."

"She's impressed with the way you took care of her," Bailey continued. "Although normally, we don't invite other guests into the honeymoon suite to use the whirlpool."

"That was a good idea," Mrs. Arbuckle said. "I should have thought of that."

"I don't want you in the Thomas Lounge tonight." Bailey took control of the conversation. "In case the Cliffords come down."

"The Cliffords." Mrs. Arbuckle laughed. "They should go fall off a cliff."

"That's enough, Maddie," Mrs. Jamieson told her friend. Then, turning to Bailey, she asked, "Now what do we do?"

"I'm thinking," Bailey said.

Mariah looked from Mrs. Jamieson to Bailey. "Aren't

you going to fire me?"

Bailey wrinkled her forehead. "Of course not." She tapped her fingers on the desk again. "However, I need to get you out of the hotel. At least for tomorrow."

"But . . . but you need help on Saturday. Tessa can't do it all."

"Poppy will do some extra shifts," Bailey said. "And tomorrow—" She paused, settling on an idea. "Tomorrow, you will go with Teague on a hike."

"I will not!"

"Yes, you will," Bailey said, matter-of-factly. "He needs help with his clients. You need to be out of the hotel."

Chapter Eight

The next morning, Mariah waited in the stairwell behind the valet station. Although she understood the need to be away from the hotel—and away from Colby and Olivia—she didn't want to go on a hike with Teague.

Except, a tiny part of her did.

Last night, Gill had delivered another tray of food to the staffroom. He told her it had been prepared especially for her by the executive chef, Guy Lafontaine, and it consisted of a large bowl of pumpkin soup with a dollop of sour cream and a sprinkle of chives on top, an egg salad sandwich on fluffy French bread, and a tall glass of milk.

Dessert was a fantastic cupcake, which tasted like it was made of graham crackers and lots of sugar and butter. Topped with marshmallow icing and sprinkled with tiny chocolate chips, it reminded her of campfire desserts of gooey roasted marshmallow and chocolate.

Now that she thought about it, there was something strange about the way she kept getting fed. It was almost as if someone were leaving food out for a stray cat.

She heard a commotion at the top of the stairs, and she saw them. Gill, Teague and that receptionist—the one from Thursday night. Roberta Smythe, that was her name.

Roberta, with her big hair and her haughty attitude and her proprietary looks at Teague. Even now, the woman rested her hand on Teague's arm as she got his attention. He said something to her, nodded and took out his cell phone. Roberta looked down the stairs, right at Mariah, as if she were a problem to be dealt with.

Of course, she *was* a problem to be dealt with. They needed to get her out of the hotel before Colby and his wife saw her. His lovely backstabbing wife.

Mariah let go of a long sigh. She hadn't seen that coming. Olivia, her best friend. The one who had delivered Colby's note on the morning of the wedding. Mariah winced, and wondered for the hundredth time how she could have been so trusting, so oblivious to what was happening. So stupid.

Feeling the presence of someone in the stairwell, Mariah turned around and saw the old gentleman from the bus. He wore the same outfit as before, and again, it looked freshly pressed. With his arms folded, he leaned against the wall and studied her.

"Did you have something to do with me not getting fired?" she asked him.

As before, he didn't say anything, but he smiled, a broad friendly smile, and then he pointed to the top of the stairs.

Mariah looked, and saw that Roberta had left. Gill and Teague were still there, and Teague was still on his cell phone.

"So?" she asked. "What am I supposed to see? Are you going to tell me—"

But he was gone, that quickly. And she hadn't heard him leave. Oh well. The old man would introduce himself when he felt like it.

She looked back up the stairs at Teague. He wore a navy T-shirt, a long-sleeved beige shirt, and beige cargo pants. His hiking boots had seen a lot of wear.

She wore similar clothes. Her light blue T-shirt, her long-sleeved white shirt and dark blue pants. All non-cotton clothing. He'd said no cotton, in case it rained, because cotton took forever to dry and therefore was not appropriate for hiking.

Bailey had supplied her with a pair of hiking boots and *rain gear*.

Fortunately, the hiking boots fit well. The rain gear—a jacket and pants in a waterproof breathable fabric—was stashed in her day pack. The rule was, you always carried this stuff, even though there was not a cloud in sight.

Or maybe it was so you had a load to carry. Rain gear, water, lunch. A kind of handicap to keep you from walking too fast.

Teague put away his cell phone and bounded down the stairs to her hiding place.

"Is the coast clear?" she asked.

"Not yet. Gill will tell us."

Bailey had arranged for this clandestine departure. Mariah had agreed, if only to keep her job. And Teague had been convinced to go along with the idea.

He stood next to her, looking up the stairs, not saying anything.

She also focused on the top of the stairs. "I'm only going because Bailey insisted."

"I know."

"And if I have to go on a hike with you, I want to go to Larch Valley."

"No, you don't."

"Yes, I do." She glanced at his profile and then returned her gaze to the top of the stairs. "It has to be Larch Valley."

"Why?"

She heard him take a long breath, and she knew he was looking at her. So she turned to him, saw that infuriatingly calm manner of his, and those blue eyes. The clearest shade of blue she'd ever seen.

Never mind his eyes, she told herself. "Because I read

that it's pretty," she said. "With the larch needles turning yellow."

His lips quirked into an almost smile. "The needles are still green. They won't turn until at least the third week of the month, more likely the last week."

"Are you sure?"

He raised an eyebrow.

Of course he was sure. She should have Googled when the larch needles turned. But she hadn't had time to find the library and a computer.

"You don't want to go there anyway," he said.

The library? Was he eavesdropping on her thoughts? Standing close to him was interfering with her concentration. "Go . . . go where?"

He squinted at her. "Larch Valley?"

Of course. She brought herself back to the moment. "Why not?"

"Because every man and his dog goes to Larch Valley."

"I didn't think you could have dogs in the National Park."

"Larch—" He stumbled on his train of thought. "You can't have dogs in the park. Well, you can if they're leashed but—forget it." He turned away, looked up the stairs, saw Gill hold up a hand, palm out.

That meant, not yet. Maybe Colby and Olivia were in the lobby. Maybe they were headed for breakfast in the Alberta Rose Coffee Shop.

"We're going to Boom Lake," Teague said.

"Boom?" Nobody named a lake, *boom*. "Is that a joke?"

"No," he said. "It's a special place."

"I'm sure it is." And she might as well give up on Larch Valley. "Why does Bailey want me to help you with your clients?"

There was a pause while he thought about what to say. "The tourist businesses always help each other out. She's worried about the way I returned Hazel Anderson."

No kidding. "So what am I supposed to do with your clients?"

He shrugged. "Put them in a whirlpool bath?"

. . . . .

Five minutes later, they stood next to the van in the hotel parking lot. Warming her back, the day pack tugged on her shoulders. Her boots felt cumbersome, and stabilizing at the same time. A slight morning breeze sifted her hair over her eyes, blinding her for a moment. She pulled her hair back and loosely braided a few loops behind her neck. Finally, she was going on a hike in the Rocky Mountains. Something she'd always wanted to do, but . . .

"I've never hiked in the mountains," she said.

"Neither had Hazel," Teague answered. "And she survived. She even enjoyed it. Mostly."

"Don't worry." Teague's assistant bounced over to where she stood, and collected her pack. He put it with the others in the back of the van.

Mariah had seen the young man by the elevator yesterday, but they had not been formally introduced.

"This is Shredder," Teague said.

"Hello, Shredder."

Almost as tall as Teague, Shredder was lean and muscular, and moving. In fact, he reminded her of the energizer bunny with his constant motion. He was probably younger than she was, probably early twenties. Like yesterday, his brown hair was tousled on top.

"Boom Lake is less than half the elevation of the Plain of Six Glaciers," Shredder told her, with a smile.

She suspected he had a perpetual smile.

"And this is Mariah," Teague said. "She likes to try new things."

Shredder squinted, frowning. "What's that?"

"Don't mind him," Mariah said. "How high will we be hiking?"

"It's an elevation gain of about five hundred feet. A bit more."

"You'll like it," Teague added.

"You have no idea what I like."

"Yes, I do."

. . . . .

The waif sat in the back of the van with the old couple from Oregon. Rolf and Suzanne had been on vacation for the past week, exploring the Banff and Kootenay Parks. Mariah appeared to be listening to them. Listening politely. As new grandparents, the old couple talked incessantly about their new grandson.

Quincy, the financial whiz kid from yesterday, was along on this trip as well. Probably because of the two university students, Jillian and Joanne. They'd come into the store yesterday evening, looking for something to do. Quincy had been there and he'd suggested this hike.

As usual, Shredder rode shotgun. "Monroe told me he was *not* doing any more bookkeeping."

Teague slumped. He'd expected as much. "I'll get someone," he said. "Soon."

"Can't you do it?"

"No."

Quincy, in the seat behind them, tapped Shredder's shoulder. "Hey, Shred. What's that mountain?"

"Castle," Shredder answered. "Castle Mountain."

"Can we climb that one?"

"Another day," Shredder answered. "We'll take the trail to Rockbound Lake. From there we can go up to Helena Ridge."

"Cool," Quincy said. He returned to his conversation with Jillian and Joanne, telling them about the hikes he'd been on, the incredible elevation gain and the near encounters with grizzlies.

Shredder, unfortunately, returned to the accounting topic. "You can't do bookkeeping? Or you won't?"

"Can't."

"Didn't they teach you anything in university?"

"I was in Kinesiology, not Commerce."

"You can do it," Shredder said. "You just don't want to."

"Right."

"I'll bet your dad could set you up with someone."

"Keep my dad out of this," Teague said, gripping the steering wheel.

. . . . .

About forty-five minutes after leaving Harmony, they arrived at the trailhead—the Boom Creek picnic area off the Banff – Windermere highway, otherwise known as Highway 93.

Except for the waif, everyone headed over to the trail sign. They needed to double-check where they'd be going, and to read the *You are here – Vous êtes ici* map.

Quincy was getting Jillian and Joanne to pose in front of the sign. Suzanne had already taken a picture of it, like she had for every trail sign she'd come across for the last week. A scrapbooking project, she'd said. Rolf had studiously refrained from comment. He simply stood where he was told.

"Why is this a special place?" the waif asked.

At the rear of the van, Shredder unloaded the day packs. "Yeah, Boss. Why is this a special place?"

Hoping the kid would not keep asking, Teague stared at

him. Then he said, "You take the fast group."

"Two groups?"

"Yes. There's no bear activity, but keep them together," Teague said. "Mariah and I will bring up the rear."

"Sure thing, Boss." Shredder trotted over to where the others waited by the trail sign.

"Bring up the rear?" The little waif was insulted. "Am I in the slow group?"

"Don't call it that," he said, seriously. "Suzanne wants to think she's a fast hiker. This is how you help."

"Pardon?" A frown wrinkled her brow and those pretty blue eyes looked puzzled.

"I'll tell Suzanne to take it easy—so *you* can keep up."

. . . . .

Mariah followed a few paces behind the older couple. After they crossed Boom Creek at the picnic area, the wide track led them up a moderate grade, and she quickly figured out just how much help the old man and woman needed.

That line about going slow for Suzanne's sake? It had only been a line. Having hiked every day for the past week, Rolf and Suzanne had plenty of stamina.

Mariah did too, she told herself. Lots of stamina, even though it was her first time hiking. Feeling her heart pounding with the constant uphill, she focused on putting one foot in front of the other. Clump. Stomp. Trudge.

Face it. This was a *lot* tiring.

Teague walked beside her, occasionally naming a plant for Suzanne. In the parking lot, Mariah had seen him speaking quietly to the older couple, no doubt arranging for them to hike slowly—but not for Suzanne.

For Mariah. If she hadn't been so out of breath, she would have sighed with the realization—Teague didn't think she could keep up. And worse, he knew she wouldn't admit it.

Was she so easy to read?

Colby had never once thought she was less capable than anyone else, and he'd never gone out of his way to take care of her.

Whoa. Where had that thought come from? Was that what Teague was doing? Taking care of her?

No one took care of her. At any rate, Colby never had. *She* had taken care of *him*, not the other way around. And, that hadn't worked out well. Had he called off the wedding because he resented her independence?

"What kind of forest is this?" Suzanne asked.

"Subalpine," Teague said. "Pretty typical. Mostly Engelmann spruce. Some alpine fir."

Rolf and Suzanne stopped often, ostensibly so that Suzanne could take a photograph of a tree or a flower or a view. Occasionally Rolf suggested a better angle for the shot, and Suzanne ignored him.

Feeling wistful, Mariah watched the older couple interact. Imagine, she thought, having a lifelong partner, someone to share your world with, someone to always be there. *If only.*

But there was no use hoping for what could not be. She was not marriage material. Her failed wedding had taught her that much.

Shaking off the gloomy thought, she focused on the day. The soft breeze, the clear sky, the amazing air. And she realized, with some surprise, that she was enjoying herself. Especially walking at this easy pace.

Shredder and Quincy and Jillian and Joanne had disappeared up the trail long ago, but the rest of them took their time, savoring these stolen moments.

To Mariah, hiking in this fresh, clean, unspoiled world was like doing something without doing anything. For a long time, her life had consisted of work, and more work.

Trying to earn a living, trying to help her mother, trying to keep the debts at bay.

Until the Fort Mac wildfires, she'd had her landscaping business. But then, all her equipment had been destroyed and her apartment had burned down. On that horrible day last May, she'd hitched a ride with one of her workers, taking what she could with her. They'd snaked out of town in the long line of traffic, until finally they'd found refuge in a high school gym where she'd been given a bowl of soup and a cot.

"Have you figured out why this is a special place?" Teague asked.

She snapped out of her unhappy past and returned to the present moment. Back to the hike. Back to the man walking beside her.

Back to this special place. Everything about this place was special . . . but she wasn't telling him that. "No," she said. "I haven't figured out why it's a special place."

He stepped ahead of her, moved a branch aside and held it out of the way, letting her pass.

"It's a special place because it's our first hike together."

She had a feeling he'd say something like that. "You are persistent."

"I know." He grinned. "Is it working?"

She almost laughed, but she stopped herself, knowing she was not getting involved with anyone. Never getting involved again. "No," she answered, and she walked on in silence, although the world was anything but silent.

She heard the cry of a bird, the swish of wings, the drone of a bee, a rustle in the underbrush, the wind murmuring in the branches of the trees. All kinds of little noises and random sounds so different from the muted clamor inside a building.

"Is this really called Boom Lake?"

"Yes, it is."

It seemed an unlikely name, after all the other names around here—Norquay, Larch, Eiffel, Fairview. Curiosity got the better of her and she had to ask. "Why pick this? For our first hike?"

He didn't answer right away, and then, "So you agree, it's our *first* hike?"

"I was speaking hypothetically."

"Of course you were." He walked a few more steps, waited for her to catch up. "I picked it because it's sheltered. It's a gradual elevation but it's more than a walk. And I like the lake. It's peaceful."

She liked peaceful, and she liked Teague, even though she knew she had to keep her distance.

And then all at once, she decided she could do that. She could keep her distance, and she could still ask questions, and she could still enjoy his company.

"How many trails do you know in the park?"

"All of them."

Again, she almost laughed. "No, you don't."

"I do," he said. "My brother and I have been hiking here since we were kids."

"You have a brother?"

He lifted his brows, a quick stare. "Lots of people have a brother," he said. "Some people have more than one."

And some people, like her, didn't have any brothers or sisters. "Do you have more than one brother?"

"One," he said. "Three years older than me." A moment of reflection. "He's done well for himself."

She heard a hint of regret in his tone. "And you, you haven't?"

"My father would say that," Teague said, firmly.

"What would you say?"

"I like what I do. I could make more money doing something else, but I like this."

"Then it's the right thing to do." She inhaled a deep

lungful of the mountain air, knowing that she liked this too. This world, this life, this man.

Better be careful, she thought, giving herself a mental shake.

After making a few more turns along the path and climbing a few more rocky steps, Teague picked up the conversation again. "What do you do?"

Long story, and not a particularly happy one. "Anything and everything."

"I know," he said. A slight pause. "What did you do before you were a maid?"

A simple answer for that one. "I worked on a cleanup crew in Fort Mac."

She'd been lucky to get a job and it had been weeks of hard labor, shoveling and sweeping, wearing a mask, living in camp. But the pay was good and she'd been able to clear her debts.

"You're back there again," Teague said.

"Yes, I was," she admitted. "And you know what's funny?"

"What?"

"The whole time I was working on cleanup, I was wondering if Colby was all right, wondering if he'd got out okay. The news said everyone did, but I worried."

A bird fluttered overhead. A dove cooed in the distance. Several feet ahead of them, they could hear the old couple laughing about something.

"I'm sorry about your wedding," Teague said. And then a second later, "No, I'm not. It gives me a chance."

Mariah shot a look at him, waited to see the humor, but there was none. It was as if he spoke seriously.

How could he do that? How could he be so, so . . . Unconstrained? "Gives you a chance?"

"I'm a nice guy," he said. "I'd never leave you at the altar."

She stopped walking and stared at him. "Are you proposing?"

He stopped walking too, turned around, took a step closer. "Do you want me to?"

"You don't know me!"

He shrugged, then he bent his head, and kissed her. A light quick touch. His lips on hers. "It only takes a few minutes to know if you like someone," he said. Then he stepped away from her, and kept walking.

Dumbfounded, she touched her fingers to her lips. It was only a playful kiss, after all. It was not serious. It was *not!*

But he was right, about the knowing. Knowing if you liked someone right away. Somehow, when she'd first seen him, it had sent a shock to her system. An instinct that told her she'd known him always.

Instinct? No. By definition, instinct was irrational. Instinct was an idiotic way to run your life.

"Come on," he called.

Trying to appear unaffected by that kiss, and by the muddle of thoughts swirling in her head, she caught up with him.

She was reading too much into this. It was simply a case of a warm September day, a break from routine, the magic of the mountains—the enormous and powerful guardians watching over the world, making it beautiful and right.

"And before you worked on the cleanup crew?" he asked.

Before? Oh yes, that conversation. Somehow they were back in that conversation. "I had a landscaping business," she said. "It burned up."

"And before that?"

She considered how much to tell him, decided there was no use hiding it. "I was a nurse."

He took a long breath, let it out. "I thought you might be."

Her glance met his eyes. Why would he think that?

"You're good with people," he said. "And Hazel Anderson thought you were a nurse." He stepped over some roots that crossed the trail. "Why don't you have a job at the hospital?"

"I don't want to work in a hospital anymore."

"No?"

"No." Careful of the bumps in front of her, she took her time. "My mother thought nursing would be a good profession. I liked it for a while. But, I'm done."

"When did you quit?"

"About three years ago." And it was best to turn this conversation around. Right now. "What did you do before you were a guide?"

Chapter Nine

Teague saw what she was doing. Flipping the conversation around to him, because she didn't want to talk about what had happened three years ago. He wondered, briefly, if he could pursue the hospital question. But he knew he couldn't, not without frightening her off. Whatever had happened, he'd find out soon enough. For now, he'd give her his story.

"Our grandfather lives in Banff, in the townsite," he said. "My brother and I spent summers with him."

"Let me guess. He took you hiking?"

"Yes. Every summer we hiked with him. We still do, sometimes."

Rolf and Suzanne had gone ahead, since they were nearing the lake. And he had an idea they were giving him some alone time with Mariah.

He continued with his story. "Then there was Camp Chief Hector, a summer camp near here. Backpacking, canoe trips, horseback riding, ropes courses."

"Outdoor survival?"

He laughed. "Survival makes it sound serious. It wasn't serious. It was fun."

"But did you learn—"

"Survival? I can survive in the wilderness, but I can do a lot more than survive."

He watched the emotions flit across her face—curiosity, sadness, maybe hope—and he had a feeling her whole life was about surviving. But they wouldn't talk about that. Not today.

"While I was in university, I needed a summer job, so I was a counselor at Camp Chief Hector."

She inclined her head. "University?"

"U of C," he said. "Kinesiology. My mother always hoped I'd go into teaching."

She nodded, walking slowly. "Is your mother a teacher?"

"Yes. Retired now."

"And your father? Is he a teacher?"

"No. He was in oil and gas. Retired now too."

She thought about that, and then, "You didn't like teaching?"

For someone who didn't want to answer questions, the waif sure had a lot of her own. "Not that I didn't like it," he told her. "I didn't want a nine-to-five."

"Did your brother?"

Teague laughed. "He went into geology. And he likes the exploration trips. But eventually, he'll end up at a desk."

They hiked a bit further and he wondered if she was out of questions. Then she said, "I'd like to end up at a desk."

From nursing to landscaping to a cleanup crew. To a desk? He shrugged. A desk would at least give her a chance to sit down. "What kind of work?"

"Management."

That would explain the online courses. "Mmm hmm."

"You didn't laugh."

"Why would I laugh?"

"Colby doesn't think I'm suited for it. He thinks I should go back to my job at the hospital."

No getting around it, Colby was an idiot. "Don't listen to Colby."

The trail had narrowed to a small footpath. Soon they

reached the large boulders that separated them from the lakeshore. "We're here," he said. "Now we have to climb over the rocks."

He reached out, holding his hand palm up. "Give me your hand."

"I can do it on my own."

Naturally, she could do it on her own. She was a survivor. He followed behind her, staying close in case she slipped.

. . . . .

They reached the lake.

Filled with tranquility, Boom Lake was beautifully formed and exceptionally clear. The green-blue water shimmered in the sunlight and reflected perfect images of the surrounding mountains. In the background, the low murmur of a soft breeze above the trees underscored the powerful sense of peace he always found here. This was a place hidden from earthly cares, a time out of time, where nothing mattered but the moment.

And, it mattered too, that she felt the same way.

The waif took in the scene, her mouth partly open and her eyes wide. She stared, and inhaled a long, slow breath, as if she were trying to pull the view deep inside herself and keep it there.

Near the middle of the lake, a fish jumped, flicked a tail and disappeared. A whisky jack touched down at the water's edge, waited a second, and took flight.

"Over there." Teague pointed. "That's Mount Quadra. And there, that's Bident Mountain."

With something like awe flooding her expression, she looked off in the distance at the glacier-topped spires.

"Turn around." He touched her shoulders, pointing her in the right direction, wanting to gather her in his arms, resisting. "That's Boom Mountain."

She laughed. A soft, musical sound. "So there's a Boom Mountain too."

"Naturally."

"Hey, Boss!" Shredder waved at them, sweeping his arm in a gesture of *come join us*.

A few moments later, they sat at the lakeshore and pulled out their lunches, lunches prepared by the Thurston Hotel kitchen—crusty buns, chunks of salami, wedges of Camembert, bunches of grapes. And of course, Guy Lafontaine's version of gorp, a mixture of raisins, almonds, big chocolate chips and sunflower seeds.

"This stuff is great," Quincy said, with his mouth full. "What is it?"

"Gorp," Shredder told him.

Quincy screwed up his face. "*Gorp?*"

"It stands for granola oats raisins and peanuts," Shredder said.

Jillian held up her bag and looked inside. "I thought it meant, good old raisins and peanuts?"

"It's that too." Shredder agreed. "And what else is it called?" He glanced at Teague.

"Scroggin. Schmogle. Depends on where in the world you are," Teague said. "In Canada, it's gorp."

Quincy studied his gorp. "This doesn't have peanuts," he said, ever literal.

"There are lots of recipes," Suzanne told him. "There are lots of different ways to do one thing."

"Whatever it's called," Rolf said, "I love Chef Guy's recipe. You can give me more of this stuff anytime."

· · · · ·

After lunch, they wandered in different directions. Quincy, always talking, escorted Jillian and Joanne along the edge of the lake. Shredder sat alone up on the rocks, getting a break from Quincy's questions. Rolf lay in the grass, sleeping. Suzanne sat beside him, scrolling through her photos. And Mariah knelt by the water. Bending over, she stared into the depths, mesmerized.

The fish, a cutthroat trout, jumped again and she heard it. As she looked away from her reflection, a necklace slipped out from under her T-shirt.

Not a necklace, more like a medallion—something circular, a little bigger than a silver dollar, with an intricate pattern of gold—antique gold—surrounding a purple stone.

"That's pretty," Teague said.

She watched the ripples expanding outward in concentric circles from where the fish had jumped. "Do you know what it is?"

"Cutthroat trout. It's pretty too, but I meant this." He touched the medallion with two fingers.

Immediately her hand gripped his, as if she were protecting something important. And then, shyly, she took her hand away, knowing he was not going to steal her necklace.

"Special?" He let go of the medallion. It swung above the water.

"Yes."

He'd seen the chain around her neck and he'd wondered if it was something she wore all the time.

"It's an amethyst." She cradled the medallion, rubbing her thumb over the purple stone. "My mother gave it to me. Her grandmother gave it to her." She tucked it back inside her shirt, and then pressed her hand over top of her shirt, and inhaled, long and deep.

"So it's an heirloom," he said, and he wondered if she would talk about it.

Lifting her head, she looked across the lake and into the

distance. "There was a story, my mother told me, when I was a little girl."

He sat down beside her on the uneven rock and shale that bordered this part of the lake.

"The story was that my mother's grandparents were married in 1938 on January twentieth. On that day, the happy husband gave this medallion," she pressed against it through her T-shirt, "to his beautiful wife."

The water lapped a bit as the wind stirred across the surface.

"My mother told me other stories about her grandparents. Apparently, she was a favorite grandchild. She loved her grandparents and they loved her."

He could hear a 'but' coming. He waited, letting her take her time.

"And then, when I got older, I figured out that if you had grandparents, you must have had parents too, and I asked about them." Mariah pulled the medallion out and held it in front of her eyes, twisting it so the amethyst sparkled in the sunlight. "But my mother never talked about her parents. And any time I asked her about them, she looked sad. So I quit asking." She tucked the medallion back inside her T-shirt. "Somewhere along the line, I realized she must have had a falling out with them, and it was one of those things that would never mend."

The wind stilled and a dark cloud fell over the water. The air felt colder. He wanted to put on his jacket. Mariah didn't seem to notice that the temperature had dropped. She knelt in her spot, wearing her T-shirt and her long-sleeved white shirt.

"My mother could have used help from her family, but she was fiercely independent. I don't think she ever wanted to ask for help."

The darkness grew, sailing across the water as clouds rose over the mountain.

"We'd better go," he said. "It looks like you'll get to use your rain gear."

"It's going to rain?"

"Good chance. Or, this high, it might snow." He could see Shredder waving to the others, assembling them to leave.

Mariah stood up on the rock. It wobbled and she stopped moving, getting her balance.

He held out his hand, lifting a brow, daring her to accept some help. He saw her chest heave, saw the debate going on inside her.

Then, she put her hand in his, and he steadied her, guiding her until she stepped onto solid ground.

"I could have done it myself," she said.

"Yes, you could have." He released her hand. "But sometimes it's nice to have help."

. . . . .

Standing in the shower, Mariah let the hot water beat over her tired muscles and take the chill out of her bones.

Bailey's rain gear would have kept her dry, if she had listened when Teague told her to pull up her hood. Instead she'd turned her face up to the beautiful cleansing rain. Of course, the rain had gone down her neck and wicked inside, soaking her clothing.

After about a half hour under the hot water, she felt better. Time to dry off and put on something warm. She changed into her other pair of jeans and her cable knit sweater. As always she tucked the medallion under her clothes.

The others were meeting in the Thomas Lounge to discuss the hike. She couldn't go, since she still had to keep out of sight. No doubt Colby and Olivia would be honeymooning, first in the Foothills Dining Room and later in the Thomas Lounge.

Collecting her wet clothes, Mariah headed down the hall to the laundry and started the load. Then she returned to the staffroom and thought about food. She should have saved some of her lunch from the hiking trip. Now, it looked like sugar cubes would have to tide her over until breakfast.

When would she get paid? In one week? Or two?

On Tuesday, she'd also be working at Dory's Clip and Curl. Maybe Dory could give her an advance. She could have asked Bailey for an advance, but Bailey had already done enough, letting her stay in the staff quarters for next to nothing. And, might as well admit it, she didn't like to ask for help, any more than her mother did.

Standing beside the table, she stared at the white fridge. Then she walked over to it, and opened it, stupidly hoping the fridge fairies had shown up.

They hadn't.

"Are you hungry?" Teague asked.

She closed the fridge and saw him standing in the doorway. "No."

"Yes, you are," he said. "I was thinking of slipping you out the back. We can leave via the loading dock."

"I'm not going anywhere."

"Excuse me! Coming through!" Gill's voice, from behind Teague.

Teague stepped into the staffroom, and Gill followed, wheeling a trolley laden with silver cloche-covered platters.

"Dinner is served," Gill said, taking a bow.

Teague looked as surprised as Mariah felt. "Is that from Guy?" he asked.

"No," Gill said. "It's from Mrs. Jamieson."

And then, wonder of wonders, Mrs. Jamieson walked in, carrying a bottle of red wine.

"I haven't had dinner yet," she announced. "You can

join me." She glanced at Teague, nodded her head, and said, "You too, Mr. Farraday."

"You want to have dinner here?" Mariah asked, wondering about those fridge fairies.

"Why not?"

"It's the staffroom," Mariah said. "You're hardly staff."

"So?" Mrs. Jamieson shrugged. "I used to manage this place. I can do whatever I want." She turned to Gill. "Gill. Go across the hall and get us four glasses."

"Four?"

"You want wine, don't you?"

"But—but I'm on duty. And I'm supposed to be near the desk."

"You have your radio. Roberta can page you if necessary. Besides, Harrison will be coming on duty soon."

Teague looked at Mariah, shrugged and pulled out a chair for Mrs. Jamieson.

She handed him the wine. "I'm sure there's still a corkscrew in there somewhere," she said, inclining her head toward the cupboards.

It didn't take long for Teague to find it.

By then, Gill had returned with four crystal wine glasses. He poured the wine, Mariah and Teague set out plates, napkin-wrapped cutlery and the platters. The feast consisted of bubbling hot lasagna, steamed asparagus with almonds, Caesar salad, toasted cheesy garlic bread, and pumpkin pie.

Halfway through dinner, Mrs. Jamieson used Gill's radio to order more wine. About five minutes later, Roberta showed up with another bottle of the CedarCreek Pinot Noir.

"Oh, Teague, honey. I didn't know you were here." She handed him the wine. "What's going on?"

"That will be all, Miss Smythe."

Roberta opened her mouth, swallowed and then

straightened. "I have a message from Bailey," she said.

"What is it?" Mrs. Jamieson asked.

"Not for you, Mrs. Jamieson. For Mariah." And then Roberta lifted her head, flounced her fluffy hair, and spoke directly to Mariah. "Bailey has a job for you tomorrow, outside of the hotel, near the bus depot."

"What is it?" Mrs. Jamieson asked, holding out her glass so Teague could refill it.

"Bookkeeping," Roberta answered, pursing her lips. "She said Mariah was qualified."

"Thank you." Mrs. Jamieson took a sip of the wine. "Bailey will give Mariah the details in the morning. That will be all."

"Humph," Roberta said, as she turned to leave. "Never heard of a maid doing bookkeeping."

. . . . .

Dinner time talk drifted from the snow at Boom Lake to the changeable weather patterns in the mountains to the time Mrs. Jamieson had been stranded with her husband, Mr. Michael Jamieson, on a hike up Cascade Mountain to the Amphitheatre.

"We took shelter under the trees as the snow fell. Back then, I had no idea it could snow in July."

"Do you still go hiking, Mrs. Jamieson?" Gill asked.

"Yes, from time to time."

"But what about your heart condition?"

"Hiking is good exercise. And more people die of heart attacks on a golf course than on a hike. Isn't that right, Mr. Farraday?"

"Yes," Teague said, "that's right. I've never lost anyone to a heart attack on a hike."

Mariah took another helping of Caesar salad. "We should take Mrs. Jamieson on a hike," she told Teague.

"Pick a time."

"I would love that," Mrs. Jamieson said. "And Mariah, would you call me . . . call me Emily?"

"Sure."

"You too, Mr. Farraday. You should call me Emily."

The matron was definitely in good spirits. And so was Mariah. Everything about today had been superb. The hike, her companions, even the rain. And now, this post-hiking celebration.

Teague held up the bottle. "More wine, Emily?"

"Please."

"Can I call you Emily?" Gill asked.

"No."

"Why not?"

"You're not related."

Mariah laughed at the non sequitur.

"Now," Emily said. "Let's clear this table. We're going to play cards."

Teague smiled and shrugged. "Works for me."

. . . . .

After they loaded the dishes onto the trolley and wiped the table, Emily Thurston Jamieson produced a deck of cards. "We'll play euchre."

Gill and Mariah had never heard of the game. Teague claimed he didn't know how to play, but he seemed to catch on quickly.

The game required two teams of two players each. Mariah teamed with Teague across the table from her, and Gill with Mrs. Jamieson. Or rather, Emily as she insisted on being called.

Mariah expected that would change tomorrow, when the wine was out of the old woman's system.

They only used the nines through the aces, making a

deck of twenty-four cards. Each player got five cards, leaving four left over and turned face down on the table.

The person who dealt turned up one of those four cards, exposing one of the four *suits*—a spade, a club, a diamond or a heart. Then, going clockwise, you had a chance to say if you wanted that suit to be *trump*. If you did, the dealer picked up the card and discarded one of his other cards, placing it face down on the unused pile.

The first rule to understand was that any card that was trump had more value than a non-trump card. As usual, an ace would beat a king would beat a queen and so on. Unless the other card in question was trump. And so, if spades were trump, the nine of spades won over an ace of hearts.

Besides that, the jacks were important. For whatever suit was trump, the jack of that suit was called the right bower and was the most powerful card in the deck. The second most powerful card was the other jack of the same color.

So if diamonds were trump, the jack of diamonds was the right bower and the jack of hearts was the left bower. Together, those two could rule a card game.

The other important thing to remember was you needed to follow suit. That's probably where the expression came from, to follow suit. If someone played a diamond and you had a diamond in your collection of cards, then you must also play a diamond. If you didn't have a diamond, you could play whatever card you wanted, although if you happened to have a card that was trump, it was usually best to play that card because you had a better chance of winning the hand.

Beyond that, Mariah didn't follow the whole thing. The scoring, for instance, seemed complicated so she let Teague do the scoring. And sometimes, it was difficult to remember which suit was trump, especially as the hour grew later and more wine was consumed.

Once during the game, Gill's pager went off and Mrs. Jamieson answered it.

It was Roberta asking for assistance with room service to the honeymoon suite on the fourth floor. Mrs. Jamieson told her to find someone in the kitchen to take care of it and to leave Gill alone.

"Thanks, Mrs. Jamieson!" Gill said. He was even more bubbly than usual, since he and Mrs. Jamieson were winning at this point. "Are you sure I can't call you Emily?"

"Yes, I'm sure. Hearts are trump." She picked up the card. "Tell me about your father, Mariah."

"My father?"

"Humor an old lady," Emily said, sorting through her cards, looking for one to discard. "Tell me about your father."

"Nothing to tell, really. I never knew him."

"Ahhh." Emily set down a card with satisfaction, looking as if she had a winning hand. "He left your mother."

"No," Mariah said, playing her ace of diamonds. "He didn't leave her. He died."

Gill followed with a king of Diamonds, Teague played a nine of Diamonds, and Emily set down her cards. "He died?"

"In a rig accident. About a month before I was born."

Emily folded both her hands over her heart. "I'm so sorry," she said, her voice shaking.

"Don't worry. It was a long time ago. Before I was even born."

But Emily did look worried. And not only worried, she looked . . . devastated. "How did Mar— How did your mother cope?"

"I think it was hard," Mariah said, watching the old lady. "But then she always worked hard and . . . Are you all right?"

"I think I'll have some more wine."

"No more wine," Teague said. "Gill, call a cab for Mrs. Jamieson."

"Emily," she corrected him.

"Okay, Emily."

Gill ordered the cab from his radio.

"You come with me, Gill," Mrs. Jamieson said. "The cab will take you home too."

"Thank you, Mrs. Jamieson," Gill said.

She got to her feet, swaying slightly. Teague took her arm.

"Let's go," she said. "We'll wait in the Margaret Library."

. . . . .

After everyone left, Mariah made herself coffee. She could have gone to bed, but she knew she wouldn't be able to sleep. Not yet. Not with all the details of this jam-packed day spinning around in her head—the hike, beautiful Boom Lake, Teague's attentiveness. And the strange way Mrs. Jamieson had been acting.

Emily, she told herself. The strange way *Emily* had been acting. For some reason the matron had taken a liking to her. To Mariah Patrick, the person without family, without connections, without much of a future—if she couldn't get on with her studies.

A loud banging in the hallway startled her.

Gill had left the trolley of dinner dishes out there. They must not have stacked them well, and something must have slipped. She checked the hall and, sure enough, she could see that one of the silver platters had fallen to the floor.

She picked it up, set it securely on the trolley, and then she saw him. The old gentleman from the bus. He stood at the end of the hall, and he waved to her.

She turned around to see if he was waving to someone else but no, she was the only one here. Curious, she walked toward him.

As she approached, he headed up the back stairs. He paused, turned to see if she was still following, she was, and he kept going up the stairs. At the top of the stairs, anyone crossing from the Foothills Dining Room to the Thomas Lounge would be able to see them.

At this point, with all the wine in her system, Mariah didn't care. So she followed the old gentleman. At the top of the stairs, he turned left, toward the executive offices.

Mariah had only been to Bailey's office, and it was in the other direction. She had not been down this way before.

At the end of the hall, a dark wood door was partially open and the light was on inside the office. The nameplate on the door said, BENJAMIN THURSTON, GENERAL MANAGER.

She hadn't met him yet, Bailey's brother, Mrs. Jamieson's—or rather, *Emily's* nephew. Vaguely, she wondered why the door was open this late at night.

The old gentleman waved his hand, inviting her to go in. She did, and there, on a huge inlaid oak desk, she found the computer, fired up and ready to use.

"Thank you," she told him. What a joyful discovery! Here at last was a computer. And so much more convenient than walking to the town's library, wherever that was. She sat in the big leather chair, opened a browser, and logged in to her statistics course.

Thirty minutes later, sleep was overtaking her. It had been a long day hiking. She'd had the wine. And she had to be up early to go to that bookkeeping job. After she finished this last exercise, she'd go to bed.

A commotion in the hallway made her look up from her work.

"There she is!" Roberta stood in the open doorway, with her hands on her hips. Behind her were two big men. One she recognized as Jason, the bartender from the Thomas Lounge. The other was a stranger. A well-dressed stranger wearing an expensive suit. His hair was neatly styled and his eyes were brown, like Bailey's.

"You can't just go into an executive office and use the computer!" Roberta shouted. "It's not like you own this hotel!"

Chapter Ten

Mariah wondered if all that wine she'd consumed with Emily was making her see things that weren't there. But the feeling only lasted a moment. She knew she was in charge of her senses. She knew that was Roberta. And she knew that was Jason, the bartender from the Thomas Lounge. Tessa had pointed him out to her on Friday, just before they'd had lunch. But, the other man?

"Who are you?" she asked.

"I'm Ben Thurston," he said. "I work here. I'm the hotel manager. Who are you?"

"Mariah Patrick," she said. "I work here too. I'm a maid."

"Nice to meet you," he said, coming around behind her. "What are you doing?"

"I'm enrolled in this Statistics course," she told him. "I'm almost finished with my assignment and then I'll be out of here."

He glanced at the screen, and then he studied it. "So you're looking for the standard deviation of that distribution?"

She snapped her fingers. "That's right! I was looking at the mean. Now if I can figure out the confidence interval for—"

"Mr. Thurston!" Roberta folded her arms. "This office was locked!"

"Who unlocked it?" Ben asked, still focusing on the

computer screen. "Try that one. There," he said, showing Mariah where she was missing her calculation.

"What's going on?" Mrs. Arbuckle rushed into the room. She wore a purple paisley robe and blue fuzzy slippers. Her white hair was set in pink curlers.

"Hello, Mrs. A," Jason said. "I thought you'd gone up to watch Jeopardy."

"I had, dear, but then Walter told me I was needed."

"Yes," Jason said, in a soft voice. "I'm sure he did."

Mariah clicked on the option Ben had shown her. The exercise closed itself and sent in her scoring. "I'm tired," she said, drowsiness seeping inside her. "I think this is enough for tonight." She got up from her chair. Or, it seemed, Ben's chair.

"Goodnight Ben," Mariah said. "It was good to finally meet you." Then she turned to Mrs. Arbuckle. "Goodnight, Mrs. Arbuckle."

"Goodnight, dear. Sleep well."

Mariah looked up at Jason . . . at *frowning* Jason.

"Do I know you?" he said.

"No," Mariah answered. "But you're Jason Knight. Tessa pointed you out to me when I started working on Friday. You've probably seen me with Tessa, doing our maid rounds."

He nodded, lips pinched, eyes squinting. "That's probably it," he said.

He looked unconvinced. As if she could have met him anywhere else. Mariah glanced at Roberta. The woman seemed upset.

"Well!" Roberta steamed. "Isn't anyone going to do anything?"

"Not me." Mariah yawned. "I'm going to bed. The computer is all yours."

. . . . .

From far away, Mariah could hear the monitor beeping, a strong steady rhythm. Someone in tachycardia. She'd better get to the patient soon, before they arrested. The last thing they needed up here was another code.

Then, close by, she smelled . . . coffee? And the beeping stopped. Had a lead fallen off? Or—oh my God—had the patient's heart stopped?!

Snapping awake, she sat up and searched the room, saw the dim light at the single window, and sitting on the bed next to her was—

"Teague?" It was Teague, looking dependable and handsome and—

"You must not have heard your alarm."

"My alarm?" Instant relief washed through her. It was only her alarm. It was only a dream. Always that dream.

"Time to get up," Teague said. He sipped the coffee. "Places to go. People to see. Bookkeeping to be done."

"Oh yes. That job." She pushed the covers back. "I have to talk to Bailey about where to go."

"I know where to go."

"You do?" She pressed her hands against her temples. "How come my head hurts so much?"

"Drink this." He gave her the mug of coffee. "You and Emily had a lot of wine last night."

Yes, now she remembered. The card game, the wine, Mrs. Jamieson. Mrs. Jamieson who wanted to be called *Emily*. Emily asking about Mariah's father, and getting so upset when she learned about the rig accident.

"Did Mrs. Jamieson get home okay?"

"Emily got home okay. Gill went with her in the cab."

Good. Hopefully she would be recovered by now. She'd looked so sad and . . . and there was one other thing. Last night . . . *oh no*, Mariah had been in the General Manager's office.

Gripping the coffee, she let go of a tight breath. That

probably had not been the best way to meet Ben Thurston.

"Hop in the shower," Teague said. "You have twenty minutes to get ready. Then I'll take you to your job."

Mariah glugged some of the coffee, felt the caffeine hit. "Why are you being so nice to me?"

"No reason," he said. "I'm nice to everybody."

"I'm not going out with you." She clutched the coffee to her chest, relishing the warmth.

"I know." He stood and headed for the door. "Twenty minutes."

. . . . .

In twenty-five minutes, she was showered and dressed. Not only that, she'd moved her laundry from the washer to the dryer. Poppy had been in the laundry room at the time, and she promised to get the clothes out of the dryer and bring them to the staffroom later in the day.

"Thanks, Poppy. You're the best."

"Hey, no worries. You'd do the same for me. Now, better run. That handsome hunk is waiting for you by the valet station."

Right, that handsome hunk. *Don't even think about it.* Mariah didn't need handsome, but she did need this job.

She wondered if her clothes were okay for this kind of work. Her jeans, her cable knit sweater. It wasn't like she had a large wardrobe to choose from. But at least, she'd mended her sweater and jacket. Thanks to Angelina, the other front desk clerk.

Mariah had bumped into her on Friday, after the ice water incident.

Angelina Fernandez was Hispanic, early twenties, and occasionally swore under her breath in Spanish. But, unlike Roberta Smythe, Angelina was friendly, kind and helpful.

When Mariah asked if the hotel had needles and thread,

Angelina had produced a sewing kit, with lots of threads to choose from. In fact, Angelina had even offered to do the mending, but of course, Mariah wouldn't let her.

So, with clothing casual but mended, she was ready for her first bookkeeping job. Skipping up the service stairs, she headed toward the valet station. As she reached the turn in the stairs, she saw Roberta standing at the top, talking to Teague.

Not exactly talking, more like preening—twirling her fingers through her hair, smiling oh so sweetly, and letting her shoulder bump against him.

He took a step back, and saw Mariah. He glanced quickly into the lobby, probably assuring that Colby and Olivia were not in view, then he waved for her to come up.

"Mariah?" Roberta squinted, looking around like she was missing something. "Now what are you doing?"

"Going for breakfast," Teague said.

"Did you know she was in Mr. Thurston's office last night?" Roberta demanded, like a school child tattling. "Using his computer!"

"Ben mentioned it," Teague said as he took Mariah's elbow. He rushed her through the mahogany and glass double doors and into the September sunshine.

"Does this mean he won't be leaving his office open tonight?" Mariah asked.

"He won't," Teague answered. "Even though you weren't hacking into his files."

"I wasn't," Mariah said. "I don't know how to do that yet."

He stopped walking, and then resumed his pace. "I didn't hear you say that."

"It's an important skill," she told him. "Businesses need white hat hackers. To test systems."

Teague stopped walking again and turned to her. "No hacking the computer where you're doing the bookkeeping, okay?"

"Okay. But why are we going this way? Bailey said the business was near the bus depot."

"It is. We're going for breakfast first."

"No." Mariah came to a halt and folded her arms. "I don't want you buying me breakfast."

"I'm not," he said. "It's a free breakfast." He touched her elbow, got her moving again.

A few minutes later they entered a bakery called *Whimsy*. A string of sleigh bells, dangling on the back of the door, announced their arrival.

"This is a bakeshop."

"Someday soon it will be a café," Teague said.

"Teague! How are you?" A pretty young woman, about five foot three with streaky ash blonde hair approached them. She was bubbly, curvy and delighted to see Teague.

Mariah felt a small pang of jealousy. Definitely not the way she wanted to feel.

"Hey, Mandy," Teague greeted her. "Nice to see you. This is Mariah Patrick. She's a maid at the Thurston."

"Hello, Mariah."

"Hello."

"I was hoping we could get a couple of your free breakfasts," Teague said.

"Sure thing." Mandy gave him a wink. "Take a seat." Then she disappeared.

Teague and Mariah pulled out chairs and sat at one of the small tables. "She winked at you," Mariah said. "What's that about?"

"Nothing."

"Something Roberta should be worried about?"

"No," he said. "Not anything for anyone to be worried about."

In a few minutes, Mandy served them scrambled eggs, toast and coffee. "Enjoy," she said, before rushing off again.

Mariah tasted the scrambled eggs. "These are delicious."

"I know."

"Have you seen Mrs. Jamieson this morning?" she asked between bites.

"No, have you?"

"No." Mariah realized she was starved. It would have been a shame to miss this breakfast. "Do you think she still wants us to call her Emily?"

"I have no idea," Teague said. He'd finished his eggs and was moving on to the toast. "She was upset last night, when she heard about your father."

"I know." As if the incident had reminded Mrs. Jamieson—*Emily*—of someone else.

"Have you tried these?" Mandy was back with two cupcakes on a white plate. The cupcakes had pink and green wrappers, and marshmallow icing sprinkled with tiny chocolate chips.

Mariah had devoured the eggs and toast. Now she tasted the cupcake. The same excellent flavor she'd had on Friday night. "Did you get these from Chef Guy?"

"Pardon?"

"I had one of these on Friday night. They're some fantastic creation from Chef Guy at the Thurston Hotel."

Mandy laughed. "*He* gets them from *me*," she said. "I make a Cupcake of the Month. That's the Summer's End S'More."

"Ahh, I see," Mariah said. "*Your* recipe?"

"Yes," Mandy answered. "I love the challenge. All you have to do is be open to possibilities."

Mariah took another bite, savored the flavor, started to wonder about— "How come you have free breakfasts?"

A slight pause. "I'm experimenting," she said. "I hope to be opening a full café soon."

"Your café will do well." Mariah swallowed her last bite

of cupcake, and eyed the one that Teague had not yet touched. "I'm looking forward to your official opening." After a moment, "And to your October cupcake."

Teague's cell rang. "I have to take this." He stood up. "It's Shredder." And then, in a lower voice, "This can't be good." He slipped outside.

Mandy came around the table and sat in Teague's chair. "You like him," she said, matter-of-factly.

"I . . ."

Mandy smiled. "It shows."

"Oh." She was not supposed to be interested in Teague. How was she messing this up so badly? "Are you . . . ?"

"We're friends. Don't worry."

"I'm not worried!"

Mandy nodded. "I like Teague. Everybody does. He's kind. He's smart. He's a great guide. But—"

"But what?"

A short pause, and Mandy smiled like she was in on a secret. "But I've never seen him get serious with anybody. Not like this."

"We're not—"

Teague rushed back inside. "We have to go," he said. And then to Mandy, "I'm taking her to a job."

"As a maid?"

"Can I take this with me?" Mariah asked, pointing to the other cupcake.

"She does bookkeeping too," Teague said. "But I hear she's a creative maid. See you later!"

Mandy handed the other cupcake to Mariah. "See you," she said. "Stay open to possibilities!"

. . . . .

In another ten minutes, they were at his store. Teague

hoped Shredder and Monroe had things under control.

"This is that place that has the Jewelry Store sign."

Right. He liked his sign. *Mountain Jewel Sports.* "Yes," he said. "The owner is looking into that." Maybe the *Sports* should have been as big as the rest of the lettering. He'd think about it, later.

As he stepped through the doorway, he saw Hazel Anderson standing on one side of the map table, and Lilith Hamilton on the other side. Lilith Hamilton—the mayor's wife and the soon-to-be mother-in-law of Brock Anderson.

Brock's father, Bill Anderson, from Calgary, sat in one of the chairs by the fireplace with Mayor Ed. They each held a mug of coffee and they seemed civil enough, but then both men were used to dealing with disputes.

For their wives, it was a different story.

"Your husband didn't want *his own* son for a partner." Lilith tossed her sleekly styled hair, lifting her chin, nose high in the air.

"It didn't seem appropriate," Hazel said. "Brock had only recently been admitted to the Bar. In a Calgary law firm, making your son a partner so soon would show favoritism."

"But it's supposed to be okay in Harmony? You don't think a Harmony law firm is as good as a Calgary law firm?"

"I'm not saying anything of the kind." Hazel faced her opponent, arms folded, feet firmly in place.

Lilith gripped the edge of the map table and leaned toward Hazel. "Brock's uncle didn't seem to have a problem making him a partner."

The door opened, and a tired-looking Emily Jamieson trudged inside. Tired, but still perfectly groomed, not a white hair out of place. What was she doing here? She rarely visited his store.

"I'm glad Reginald could find a position for Brock,"

Hazel said, her tone measured and reasonable.

"But," Lilith stabbed her finger across the table, "you don't think he's good enough to be a partner."

"I didn't say that."

"You implied it." More finger poking. "You don't think *your own* son is good enough to be a partner. Well, I don't think he's good enough to marry my daughter!"

Hazel sighed, and stared at Lilith. "You make small towns seem so provincial."

Glancing away, Lilith noticed Teague, and he had second thoughts about walking into the mix. Never tangle with a mother bear if her cubs are involved.

"Mr. Farraday!" Lilith shouted. "Your father offered to help you, didn't he?"

"I didn't want his help." As soon as he said it, he realized it was the wrong answer—for this situation. In his case, not accepting help had been the right decision. Teague knew he could make it on his own and that's the way he wanted it.

"You see? Mr. Farraday didn't need any help. He didn't accept handouts."

"Neither did Brock," Teague said. "In fact, he accepted more responsibility by taking on a partnership role."

"You stay out of this!" Lilith shrieked at him.

And then Mrs. Jamieson, *the* Mrs. Emily Thurston Jamieson, took charge. "Lilith! What is the matter with you? Your daughter is in love with Brock. Stop interfering with her wedding."

"I'm not interfering. I'm protecting her!"

"Brock Anderson is a perfectly good choice for a husband," Emily said. "And even if he wasn't, it's none of your business. Stay out of Riley's affairs, or you may lose her."

"Lose her? *You* should talk, Ms. High and Mighty." Infuriated now, Lilith practically spat out the words. "I've heard about *your* daughter."

Her daughter? That was news to Teague. *Emily had a daughter?*

"You drove her away with your interfering!"

The store fell silent. The other customers didn't even pretend to not be listening. Bill Anderson and Ed Hamilton squirmed in their chairs beside the fireplace. Then Ed attempted to change the mood. "The weather seems as if—"

"Exactly." Emily Thurston Jamieson drew herself up tall. "I made a mistake. Don't you make the same one." She glared down at the woman. "Now get out of here. Go home and find something useful to do."

"Well!" Lilith sucked in air, so full of rage she trembled. "I'm not sure I want my daughter's reception at your hotel. I'm not sure I want to be dealing with you at all, Mrs. Jamieson."

Finally, Mayor Ed stepped up. "I am sure," he said, scowling at his wife.

"We're going for a walk," Teague announced. "Ladies?" He motioned to Hazel and Lilith and waved his hand toward the door.

"I don't want to walk," Lilith pouted.

"Along Harmony Creek," Teague said. "It's a pleasant stroll."

"I hiked to the top of the Plain of Six Glaciers," Hazel said. "Can't you even manage a little walk along the creek?"

"Of course I can. I've done it a million times."

Teague knew she'd done it once. Maybe twice. He also knew a little exercise might calm them down. In fact, he would walk them until they couldn't talk any more.

Teague looked around. "Monroe?"

Monroe looked up from where he was crouching behind the register.

"Get some coffee for Mrs. Jamieson," Teague said.

"Then show Mariah the books."

Holding her cupcake in both hands, Mariah blinked. She'd soon figure out it was his shop. Hopefully, she wouldn't make a fuss about him helping her.

In fact, if she really could do bookkeeping, *she* was the one who would be helping *him*, not the other way around.

"Ladies." He held the door open, and waited until Hazel and Lilith walked outside.

Chapter Eleven

Emily had a daughter?

"Are you all right?" Mariah whisked over to Mrs. Jamieson.

Last night the old woman had been upset when Mariah had mentioned the death of her father. And now this. She had a daughter? An *absent* daughter?

"Yes, Mariah, I'm fine," Mrs. Jamieson said. "I will be anyway. Now you go do your job. I don't want to interrupt your work."

"Mrs. Jamieson, if you'd like I can walk with you back to the hotel?"

"Emily," she said, gently.

"Emily." So *Emily* was still what she wanted to be called.

Shredder approached. "Would you like some coffee? Tea?"

"I'll go to the hotel. I want to see Maddie." And then, "Mrs. Arbuckle," she clarified. "Let me know when you get back to the hotel, Mariah. I'd like to have lunch with you."

"I don't think I'm supposed to be visible at the hotel in case . . . you know . . . Colby."

"Don't worry about Colby. If he checks out, it's his loss." Taking a deep breath, she straightened her shoulders, turned around. "Shredder?" She faced him. "Is that really your name?"

"Yes, Mrs. Jamieson, it sure is."

"Very well, Shredder. Would you please call me a cab?"

Shredder picked up the phone and Mrs. Jamieson marched to the door.

As usual, she looked strong and in charge, but . . . maybe a little less so.

Emily. Emily who had a daughter. Somewhere.

"Well, that was interesting," the man named Monroe said.

Shredder set down the phone, finished with his call. "Just a usual day around here." He shrugged.

Monroe thought about it, nodded, and swung his attention to Mariah. "This way." He headed toward the back corner of the store. "Bring your cupcake," he said. "There's coffee upstairs."

Monroe was tall, lean, athletic. Like Teague, only not quite as tall. His dark brown curly hair trailed on his collar and his face was framed by a closely trimmed mustache and beard.

Mariah followed him past the corner fireplace where two older men still sat, presumably the husbands of Hazel and Lilith.

She guessed that Mayor Ed was the one with the black glasses and the big smile. He wore a white shirt open at the collar, a black sports jacket and casual beige trousers. He was a person who would diffuse arguments.

The other man, the more subdued gentleman, would be Bill Anderson, the lawyer. He wore a navy suit, a blue shirt and a navy tie. He wouldn't smooth over arguments. He would resolve them.

"Coming?" Monroe waited for her.

She followed him through the archway into what appeared to be a storage room. To her right, shelving held dozens of various sized boxes.

At the back, also to her right, rows of kayaks lined the

wall, and next to them hung life jackets and paddles and different lengths of bungee cords. In the center of the back wall was a large overhead door. This must be a loading area for merchandise coming into the store.

"This way." Monroe headed toward a silver metal spiral staircase in the back left corner of the room.

When they arrived on the second floor, Mariah was surprised by how brightly lit it was. Six wide windows overlooked the alley. A long couch backed onto that wall, across from a huge widescreen television.

Monroe opened a door which led to the front room, a room as large as the store below.

A twin of the store's fireplace was in the corner on her right as she entered. To her left was a long counter which ended in an L. The countertop was gray granite with the usual stovetop, dishwasher, sink and fridge. All stainless steel appliances. Nothing on the counter except for a coffee maker with a full pot of coffee.

Across from the counter was an island, with the same granite countertop, and with four tall chairs on the other side. The island held a laptop computer, a landline, and heaps of papers.

Beyond that was a large open area, with more wide windows across the front of the room. A few big plants stood in the sunlight from the windows.

In the right corner at the front, a large black oval rug filled much of the space. The far left corner of the room contained a king-sized bed—its dark blue sheets tucked with military precision.

Except for the bed, the four chairs by the island, and two upholstered chairs in front of the fireplace, the room had no other furniture.

Mariah walked around the island to get a look at the laptop, a large machine with probably a fifteen-inch monitor. It sat ready, an Excel spreadsheet opened.

She considered the stacks of papers scattered over the island's shiny granite. At a quick glance, they looked like receipts, invoices, bank statements and bills. There was also a legal-size pad of yellow paper, a small calculator, two ballpoint pens and a yellow pencil snapped in half.

"Bathroom's through that door." Monroe pointed to a door to the left of the bed.

"Someone lives here?"

"The owner," Monroe said. "He hates bookkeeping and he's the last one to have anything to do with this." He gestured, with a grimace, toward the laptop and the stacks of papers. "He used to have me do the books, but it didn't work out." Then, perhaps to be encouraging, he said, "Coffee's fresh. Call me—dial 0 on the phone—if you have any questions."

And before she could think of one, Monroe left.

· · · · ·

After about two hours of meandering along Harmony Creek, it became apparent that neither Hazel nor Lilith was going to admit she was getting tired.

But, at least, they had stopped talking about their children and the wedding. Conversation had focused on less contentious topics.

Was the Foothills Dining Room at the Thurston up to Calgary standards? It was. Did the local Sleek Chic have a good enough selection of dresses? It did. Were Teague's hiking tours to the mountains outrageously expensive? Of course not.

They agreed on those things, but on most topics, Lilith quarreled.

When the town hall renovations came up, Hazel praised the work and Lilith found points to criticize. When they talked about Whimsy's cupcakes, Hazel insisted they were the best she'd ever tasted, and Lilith refused to say a good word about the bakery. Teague suspected there'd been an argument with Mandy Brighton about the wedding cake design, or the ingredients. Or both.

When they started talking about the Tea Shop and the Wiccan fortune teller who worked there, it was a surprise to hear them both agree that predicting the future by the leftover leaves in a tea cup—or by any other means—was nonsense.

And that was when Teague had herded them back to the Thurston.

· · · · ·

He followed them through the big double doors, past the valet station and to the door of the Margaret Library.

Hazel said she would wait there for her husband and while she was waiting she would deal with some messages on her phone.

Lilith had other things to do. With a stiff but polite goodbye, she left them and headed to the Foothills Dining Room. Although the wedding was not until December, she needed to see Chef Guy, right away, to discuss a point on the menu.

"Teague, honey! Are you here for lunch?"

Roberta had spotted him from her post at the reception desk.

"Angelina will be relieving me in a half hour. Why don't we have lunch together? We can meet at the Thomas Lounge."

Before Teague could come up with a decent reply, Jason Knight came out of the Peaks Bar.

"Hey," he said. "I want to talk to you."

Teague needed to get back to the store. Or maybe not. It might be better to stay out of Mariah's way while she sorted through his accounting mess. "Talk to me about what?"

"Had lunch?"

"Not yet."

"Come to the Lounge," Jason offered. "I'll get you a steak sandwich." And, as he passed the reception desk, "Hi, Roberta."

. . . . .

In a few moments, they walked into the Thomas Lounge.

Mrs. Jamieson sat with Mrs. Arbuckle at one of the small tables near the bar. With their heads angled close together, they were probably discussing their latest soap opera episode.

Remembering last night's card game, he wondered if she still wanted to be called *Emily*. "Hello, Emily," he said, as he walked by.

"Hello, Teague," she answered. "Is Mariah working on your books?"

"Yes, she is."

"Do make sure she gets some lunch?"

"I've already arranged it." Monroe would bring up sandwiches at noon, if Mariah was still there. He wouldn't be surprised if she'd given up. Everyone else had.

Teague chose one of the seats near the middle of the bar, a few paces away from where the old ladies sat. Jason dealt with a lone customer at the end of the bar. Then he brought Teague a bottle of water.

"Your order will be out in a few minutes."

Mrs. Jamieson and Mrs. Arbuckle slipped back into their conversation.

"You have to tell her," Mrs. Arbuckle urged.

"She'll hate me," Mrs. Jamieson said.

Hate me? He wouldn't be surprised since he knew the woman could be blunt. Maybe she'd said something else to Lilith Hamilton . . .

Good for Emily, he thought, smiling.

"Who is she?" Jason asked.

Teague brought his attention back to the bar. "Who are you talking about?"

"Your girlfriend. The pretty girl with the reddish brown hair. I finally met her last night."

As he heard the words, Teague felt his hands tighten, felt a flare of jealousy. Completely unnecessary, since Jason was in a committed relationship.

"She was in Ben's office," Jason said. "Using his computer."

"I heard about that." Mariah had been a little tipsy with all that wine at the card game. "She's not my girlfriend," he said, as she kept telling him.

Jason stared at him. "But you're working on it."

No use denying it, Teague thought. His chest slumped. "Yeah."

"Good man," Jason said. "So, who is she?"

"Mariah Patrick."

"I know her name, but . . ." He stood there, across the bar, palms up and open.

"But what?"

"I've met her somewhere." He looked up at the ceiling, searching through memories.

Teague narrowed his eyes. "You have? Where?"

"That's just it," Jason said, a slight frown, head cocked. "I can't remember."

Humph. "You're mistaking her for someone else?"

"I'm a bartender. I remember faces. And I remember her face."

Teague sighed, feeling that wisp of jealousy again. "You've gone out with her?"

"Get serious. If I had gone out with *her*, I would have remembered."

Again, Teague had to tell himself not to worry. In no way was Jason competition.

After a few moments, Teague let go of his concern, knowing Jason would eventually figure out the connection. It would be a funny story, and they would both laugh. But for now, although Teague was not a person to gossip, he needed to know about Mrs. Jami— About *Emily*. He didn't know why, but she had taken an interest in Mariah, and if Emily cared about Mariah, he cared about Emily.

Leaning across the bar, he got Jason's attention.

"Did you know Emily Jamieson has a daughter?" he asked in a low voice.

Jason flicked a glance to the table behind Teague, where the person in question sat deep in conversation with her friend. "It's not something she likes to talk about."

So it was true. Teague had always thought Emily was childless. But then he'd only lived in Harmony for about ten years.

"If she'd had a daughter—" He did the math. "The daughter would probably be in her fifties now."

"That's right."

"And the daughter might have children of her own."

"Maybe."

"What happened?"

Jason watched him a moment, and then must have decided it was okay to tell Teague.

"The daughter was eighteen and wanted to get married," Jason said. "Mrs. Jamieson wouldn't permit it. So the daughter threatened to elope." He paused, let that sink in. "Mrs. Jamieson told her not to come crawling back when she needed money."

"Harsh."

"It's doubtful she meant it. She was angry. But the

daughter heard it and, so far, she's never come back."

There was silence for a couple of beats. "That's sad," Teague said.

"Yeah."

Did anyone know what had happened to the daughter? He waited for Jason to tell him more, but Jason seemed distracted.

After a moment, Jason said, "It was a formal occasion."

Formal? The mother and daughter had split up at some formal occasion? "What formal occasion?"

"Mariah. When I met her," Jason said. "She had her hair up." He held his hands around his head, fingers stretched up. "You know? How they pile their hair up for special occasions?"

Teague sighed, wishing Jason would concentrate on one thing at a time. And that thing about formal? Mariah at a formal occasion didn't make sense. She didn't strike him that way. Not the person who was happy to be a maid. Not the person who'd worked on the cleanup crew at Fort Mac.

But then, she'd also been a nurse. Who knew what else she'd done?

"It'll come to me." Jason said, and he left to serve another customer.

· · · · ·

Mariah had been entering data for hours and now it was almost three o'clock. Monroe had brought sandwiches at noon, made a fresh pot of coffee, and left her alone, perhaps afraid to interrupt her forward momentum.

She'd needed to correct a few entries. There'd been some dates and amounts mixed up, numbers transposed, entries duplicated. But nothing she couldn't fix. Once she had it sorted out, it should be easy to maintain.

For now, she needed a break. She'd have another cup

of coffee, and eat that last sandwich. She wished she could have another *cupcake*. But, if this worked out, she'd have three jobs. The maid job, the job at Dory's Cut and Curl, and this bookkeeping job. And then she'd be able to afford cupcakes. Life was good.

After pouring her coffee, she wandered across the room to the front windows. She was looking down on Main Street, and the old-fashioned black lamp posts and the baskets of late season flowers hanging from them. For the whole distance from the bus depot to the Thurston Hotel, Main Street only had businesses on this side. The view from the second floor of Mountain Jewel Sports was of Harmony Creek and the park along it.

Since she'd arrived three days ago, there hadn't been time to explore the town, and she hadn't realized how pretty it was. She sipped the hot coffee and let her mind wander.

Three days. Getting a job so quickly. Almost losing it when Colby and Olivia had shown up. Hiking yesterday at Boom Lake . . . where Teague had kissed her.

Did she want something more with him?

No. It was not the right time. She needed to move on from—

Colby? Well, she'd certainly done that. As far as occupying her thinking, he was gone like a wisp of smoke. But she still felt too unsettled for another relationship. She needed time.

She sipped more coffee and watched the street, the locals and tourists spending time in the September sunshine.

Three middle-aged women sat on a bench in the park. An older man walked a Labradoodle. Two young girls, very likely twins, bounced along the sidewalk, happy and carefree. Their hair was long, straight and brown, and she guessed they were about thirteen years old. A group of boys sped by on their bicycles. A young mother walked with her daughter, holding the little girl's hand, a pretty little girl about five or six years old.

Poor Emily. What had happened to *her* daughter?

Mariah sighed. It must have been a serious falling-out. A bad misunderstanding, where things were said that should not have been said in hasty angry moments. Thinking about it now, Mariah suspected that Emily's daughter had been as strong-willed as Emily.

A wave of sadness washed over her, a bittersweet reminder of Mariah's *own* mother. Her mother had had issues with her parents too. Issues that had never healed.

What a tragedy. Both for her mother and for Emily Jamieson.

Mariah pressed her hand over her heart, feeling the medallion under her clothes. Her mother's medallion.

Oh well, what was done was done. At any rate, it was time to get back to work.

There was one more stack of papers to deal with. Mostly receipts and invoices, but mixed in with them, Mariah found a warranty for an avalanche beacon, five canceled movie stubs, a scribbled grocery list, a copy of *Whitewater Paddling*, and an empty envelope addressed to Teague Farraday, Mountain Jewel Sports, Harmony, Alberta.

She studied the envelope. A Banff, Alberta postmark. Teague had said his grandfather lived in the town of Banff so this would be from his grandfather. Only a grandfather would send a *real* letter. But what was this envelope doing with these papers?

She shrugged and set it aside. Teague must have left it at the store when he'd met a group to guide. Assuming the guiding happened out of this store.

Then she remembered the kayaks and life jackets lined up downstairs. Teague's guiding *was* based out of this store.

He probably had some kind of deal with the owner.

. . . . .

When Teague finally made it back, Monroe was at the cash register, chatting with a customer and finishing off a sale. Shredder was at the back wall, arguing with a customer about the right choice of backpack. Teague pressed his fingers to his forehead and briefly closed his eyes.

The kid meant well, but he needed to develop some sales skills. Then again, maybe he never would. Shredder liked guiding, not sales. Maybe it would be best to keep him on as a guide and find someone who liked selling.

"Hey, Boss," Shredder called to him, abandoning the customer. "We have eight tourists signed up for the rafting trip tomorrow."

That was good news. Plus, it would be fun. Teague loved taking tourists down the Kan, and the store could use the income.

"Do I have to sit with the gorbies?" Shredder asked, a pleading look on his face.

Last trip, Shredder had sat in the raft and been completely out of place. "No," Teague answered. "You can kayak alongside and pick up anyone who falls out."

"Sweet." Shredder immediately cheered up. "I'll do some rodeo for them at the Hollywood Hole."

"Just don't tell them they're all going to die."

"It makes them scared," Shredder said. "They want to be scared."

Teague wasn't so sure about that. At any rate, having Shredder show off in a kayak might result in someone wanting kayaking lessons.

"Let's hope nobody jumps out when we go over the Widowmaker," Shredder said. "It took forever to get that guy off the rocks last time."

The poor guy had panicked. Convincing him to jump back in had been impossible, and Shredder had to pry him off and swim him across. No one had been in danger, but they thought it was dangerous and that had made for a lively group in the Thomas Lounge that night.

Monroe had taken over with the backpack customer and was listening to what the guy wanted. Nothing for a long trip, nothing for backcountry. Rather, a simple pack for city use. Monroe was always great with the customers.

And Shredder was becoming an excellent guide. If only someone could handle the numbers, life would be perfect.

"Is Mariah still upstairs?"

"She sent me out for file folders," Shredder said. "And she told me to order some red bear bells."

"Bear bells? We have lots of bear bells."

"She said to get red ones. Green ones too. She thinks people will buy them for Christmas ornaments. A souvenir from Harmony."

"Red and green bear bells." *What next?*

"But other than that she hasn't come down," Shredder said, as he collected flower identification books off the map table and carried them to the bookcase. "She's either getting through that mess or she's fallen asleep."

It was time to find out. Teague set his shoulders and headed for the stairs. Half a minute later, he entered his quiet apartment and discovered that, for the first time in months, the island was clear of papers—except for a fat accordion file.

Had she entered everything? Already? And where was she? The chairs by the fireplace were empty. Was she in the bathroom? No—

Sound asleep, she was curled up like a cat on the end of his bed, her hair fanned over the blanket, her hands tucked under her cheek.

He wasn't surprised. She'd looked exhausted when she'd stepped off that bus on Thursday. Then she'd worked all day Friday, hiked for the first time yesterday, and she'd been up late last night with Emily and her card game. And then a whole day of entering numbers. No wonder she was worn out.

Careful not to shake the bed, he stretched out beside her and watched her sleep, feeling a peace he'd never felt before. Something about her drew him like a migrating bird on its way home.

Her lashes fluttered and her eyes opened, and she looked back at him with a dreamy look in those beautiful blue eyes. And then—

"Oh my God!" She bolted upright and fell off the end of the bed.

"Hey, don't mind me." He leaned over the end of the bed and looked down at her. "You can keep sleeping."

"I can't sleep here!" She staggered to her feet, combing her fingers through her hair. "What if the owner came home!"

"Don't worry about it. He's a nice guy," Teague said. He got up off the bed, walked to the island, peeked inside the accordion file. "Did you actually enter all that stuff?"

"It's finished," she said, coming closer.

"It is?"

"It's simple bookkeeping."

Right. Simple.

"Please don't say anything about me falling asleep. I'd never get hired."

He leaned in and kissed her. "You're hired."

It had been spontaneous, the kiss. And now he wanted to take her in his arms, kiss her again, more thoroughly this time.

She didn't look like she'd mind. Her eyes grew dark and enchanting. She touched his arm, moved closer—

And then Shredder breezed into the room. "Hey, Boss! Where do you want me to put the shipment of ski boots?"

Teague jerked back, faced his employee, and felt like punching him. "Leave them in the back for now. We need to reorganize that ski section."

"Sure thing, Boss." Shredder disappeared.

The room was quiet again. Teague turned around.

Mariah was staring at him. "*You* own this store."

"I own this store. Along with my guiding business."

She folded her arms. "I see."

Something about the way she said that . . . "You see what?"

"You invented this job," she said. "For me."

"No. I didn't. I need help with the books."

"Then why didn't you tell me it was your business?"

He drew in a deep breath, let it out. "Because I thought you'd make a fuss about me helping you. And you . . ." He ran his hands over his head. Best not to finish that thought.

"Yes. I am making a fuss," she said. "You don't have to invent a job for me. I can find my own job. I don't need any help."

Chapter Twelve

After leaving Mountain Jewel Sports—Teague's store—Mariah made up her mind not to accept any payment for the bookkeeping. It had been easy work and there must be lots of bookkeepers in this town who could do it. Teague was obviously trying to help her, trying to take care of her.

She needed to take care of herself.

Pushing through the big double doors of the Thurston Hotel, she caught a glimpse of Roberta at the reception desk. At least, there was no sign of Colby or Olivia.

Olivia. Mariah shook her head. Olivia, who had pretended to be her friend, who had pretended to care about her. Olivia had even been there when Mariah had bought the dress. Oddly, Olivia's betrayal felt worse than Colby's.

Taking the service stairs behind the valet station, Mariah headed for the staffroom and the green lockers. In a minute, she'd opened her locker, pulled out the garment bag she'd carted around since January, and carried it to her cot.

Her freshly laundered clothes were there, neatly folded. Poppy, as promised, had done that. Poppy, who hardly knew her was being kind to her.

And Teague? Was he being kind? Giving her that job? And had she just thrown it in his face?

Okay, so she had a few issues to work out. But not

right now. Now she would finally deal with this dress.

As she unzipped the silver bag, billows of lace, tulle and silk spilled onto her cot.

She shook out the dress. The unused, very expensive wedding dress.

Floor length and white, the dress was romantic and graceful with an off the shoulder neckline, a full skirt of tulle-covered silk, and sheer long sleeves made of tulle and lace.

Mariah laughed at herself. Perhaps she had fallen in love with the dress, more than she had fallen in love with Colby. Maybe she had simply fallen in love with the idea of being in love and she had tried to make Colby be her Prince Charming.

Okay, so she was not a good judge of character. All the more reason to stay away from Teague before she fell in love with him.

Fell in love?

No. Not going to happen. She would *not* let that happen. Whatever she felt for Teague, it was different than what she'd felt for Colby. But right now, she simply felt irritated.

A thought popped into her head. She had never felt irritated with Colby. Not once since she'd met him. It had all been perfect—right up until it had not been anything at all.

Only a pile of lace and tulle and silk.

. . . . .

With the wedding dress tucked back into its garment bag, Mariah ran up the stairs. No way did she want Colby or Olivia to catch her on the elevator. Besides, the stairs were faster.

As she reached the sixth floor, she heard the elevator

ding, so she waited at the turn in the stairwell. No one came out of the elevator. It must have been someone going down.

She checked the hall and found it empty. Then the lights flickered. What was it with those lights?

Clutching the garment bag, she walked firmly to Suite One. As she lifted her hand to knock, the door opened.

"Hello, dear. How are you?"

"Mrs. Arbuckle. Are you on your way out?"

"No, I was just having tea. Come in," Mrs. Arbuckle said, holding the door. "Sit, Betty Jo."

Mrs. Arbuckle's little fluff-ball of a dog trotted to a mat near the window, spun in a circle, and curled up to sleep.

"What have you got there?" Mrs. Arbuckle asked, eyeing the garment bag.

Mariah stepped into the suite—the mostly *white* suite. Walls, drapes, the ceiling with its Tudor beams, all were white. The couch and chairs were white, and a white tablecloth covered the round table near the windows. The floor was golden hardwood with a light pinkish tapestry carpet in front of the fireplace. The hearth was black, but the mantel and the fireplace surround were also white.

The rest of the room had accents of gold and green. Gold in the picture frames and mirrors. Green in the bushy green plants.

Taking a moment, Mariah let herself absorb the room's calmness, and then she unzipped the garment bag and fluffed out the dress. Arranging it on the back of the couch, she said, "This was supposed to be my wedding dress."

Mrs. Arbuckle studied the silky, tulle-covered material. "It's beautiful." She looked at Mariah. "And you're not sure what to do with it."

"I'll never use it."

"You'll get married someday."

"I might. But even if I do, it won't be in this dress."

Mrs. Arbuckle nodded. "Would you like me to sell it for you?"

"No," Mariah answered. "I want to give it away. I thought maybe *you* could give it away. Anonymously." She hadn't quite sorted through the idea. "Somebody is going to want to get married. And they might need a dress. And . . . I mean . . . well, people often inherit wedding dresses. Somebody could inherit this one."

"That's a wonderful idea!" Mrs. Arbuckle beamed. "I don't know anyone offhand, but I'm sure an opportunity will come up." She leaned down and brushed the soft tulle, sifting the material in her fingers.

"I was supposed to get married last January," Mariah said. "So the dress is for a winter wedding. But it could be for any season, I suppose."

"There will no doubt be a winter wedding that needs it," Mrs. Arbuckle said, confidently. "They will want to thank you."

"No. I want to give it anonymously. I hope it makes some bride happy. That's the only thanks I want."

"All right then," Mrs. Arbuckle agreed. "That's what we'll do."

Details taken care of, Mrs. Arbuckle straightened, pivoted and walked to the fireplace. "Now tell me about that nice young man."

"Nice young man?"

"Teague Farraday." A knowing smile lit her face. "How did your bookkeeping job go?"

Naturally, Mrs. Arbuckle would know about that. Emily would have told her. No doubt, everyone in the hotel knew about that job. Probably everyone in Harmony.

"It wasn't really a job."

Mrs. Arbuckle frowned. "How do you mean?"

"It's his store. He owns Mountain Jewel Sports. Did you know that?"

"Everyone knows that, dear."

Of course they did. "He pretended he needed someone to do his accounting."

"I think he does—"

Mariah sighed, and switched gears. "He's trying to take care of me."

Mrs. Arbuckle tilted her head, blinked. "Is that a bad thing?"

"I can't depend on someone to take care of me. I need to be able to take care of myself."

"Yes." Mrs. Arbuckle nodded and pressed her lips together. "There seems to be a lot of that going around."

A lot of—? That made no sense. "I'd better go," Mariah said. She turned toward the door, and stopped.

The dress was taken care of. She still needed to figure out what was going on with Teague. But she also needed to know what was happening with Emily. And, if anyone knew anything, it would be Mrs. Arbuckle.

"Have you seen Mrs. Jamieson today?"

"Not yet. Why?"

How much should she repeat? On second thought, did it matter? This morning, every customer in Mountain Jewel Sports had heard. It was only a matter of time until Mrs. Arbuckle heard too.

"This morning, Lilith Hamilton was shouting at Mrs. Jamieson."

With a twinkle in her eye, Mrs. Arbuckle adjusted the position of a shiny gold-framed photograph on the mantel. "That's nothing new, dear. Lilith shouts at everyone."

"She said that Mrs. Jamieson had a daughter."

Mrs. Arbuckle nodded, slowly, and walked toward the couch.

"You knew that," Mariah said.

"Yes." Mrs. Arbuckle leaned down, inspecting the dress again.

"And last night Emily was upset."

"Emily?" She turned around.

"She wants me to call her *Emily*."

That got a big smile from Mrs. Arbuckle. "Yes, she would like that. Mrs. Jamieson is much too formal for your relationship."

"My *relationship*?"

"Yes, well, what was she upset about?"

"My father."

"Hmmm. Your father. Yes." Mrs. Arbuckle stalled, perhaps finally hearing some *new* information. "What did you tell her about your father?"

"That he died."

Mrs. Arbuckle's hand went to her heart and she sank to the couch, sitting beside the wedding dress.

"It was a long time ago," Mariah said, rushing to the woman. "Before I was even born. About a month before I was born. A rig accident."

"Then . . . your mother . . . she was all alone," Mrs. Arbuckle said, her voice low. "Poor Mary."

Mary? "How did you know her name was Mary?"

"Why . . ." Mrs. Arbuckle shook her head, recovering somewhat. "I thought you told me."

Mariah shrugged, trying to remember what she'd said. "Yes, Mary. That's why she called me Mariah, because it's like her name." Mariah was babbling now, as she watched Mrs. Arbuckle to see if she might be having a stroke or a heart attack. "She gave me Margaret for a middle name, because that was my mother's grandmother's name." Good. Mrs. Arbuckle's color was improving.

"I see," Mrs. Arbuckle sat up straight.

She seemed perfectly fine again, and Mariah wondered if she had imagined the woman going pale. "Anyway, I was worried about Emily. Because she seemed so upset. Both about my father. And by what Lilith said."

A knock sounded on the door.

Spry as ever, Mrs. Arbuckle leapt up from the couch and went to open it.

"Hi, Mrs. Arbuckle," Gill said. "I was looking for—oh! There you are. I was looking for you, Mariah." He bobbed on his feet. "Mrs. Jamieson is waiting for you in the Alberta Rose Coffee Shop."

. . . . .

Ten minutes later, Mariah was crossing the lobby. Gill had said he'd stop in to walk Mrs. Arbuckle's little dog in about an hour, and he would check on Mrs. Arbuckle at the same time.

Gill had also mentioned that Teague was looking for her. Apparently he was in the Thomas Lounge talking to Jason the bartender.

What to do about Teague? She liked him, perhaps too much. And yes, she'd probably overreacted. But she couldn't have him inventing a job for her. She would see what Emily wanted and then she would talk to him.

"Mrs. Jamieson is in the Coffee Shop," Roberta hollered, from her post behind the reception desk. "She wants to see you. Now."

It sounded like an order. Like being sent to the principal's office. Someone needed to talk to Roberta about tact. At least, there weren't any guests in the lobby.

Mariah found Mrs. Jamieson—*Emily*—sitting at one of the small tables that faced the courtyard.

"Mariah, I'm glad you could come," she said, as Mariah took the chair opposite.

Greta approached them, her long hair swaying, her smile genuine.

"Hello again, Mariah. Mrs. Jamieson. Can I bring you anything?"

"You did have lunch, didn't you?" Emily asked, a slight worry in her tone.

"Yes, I did. Thanks."

"Would you like coffee then? Or tea?"

"Whatever you're having will be fine."

"Tea, Greta. The Earl Grey. And some of Guy's crème caramel."

From where Mariah sat, she faced the Coffee Shop. If Colby came in, she could duck under the table. She didn't want to cause Bailey any more trouble and being here was not a good idea. But, it wasn't like she could object to where Emily wanted to meet.

"Mariah, there's something I need to tell you."

"I know," Mariah said. "Teague owns Mountain Jewel Sports."

"Pardon?"

"You wanted to tell me that you found out it wasn't an actual job."

"Really?"

"He's trying to take care of me."

"*Is* he now?"

For some reason, Emily was smiling, broadly.

"There's nothing wrong with wanting to take care of yourself," Mariah insisted.

"No, of course not."

"It's a good way to be. Then no one can ever let you down. That's what my mother always said."

Emily's smile disappeared. Somehow, she seemed sad. "Well . . ."

It was as if she had something to say but didn't know where to start. Emily had come across as in charge, direct and not one to mince words. However, that's what she was doing now. Mincing words. Or at least choosing them carefully.

Then she seemed to change course.

"As far as Teague goes," Emily said, confident now, "you need to be willing to let someone take care of you."

Mariah angled her head. "Are you giving me advice?"

"Oh dear, I was, wasn't I? Heaven knows I shouldn't do that." For a second, Emily seemed flustered. Then she let it go. "Never mind him taking care of you," she said. "You can take care of him."

Mariah laughed, quick and hollow. "How could I possibly do that?"

"He needs help managing that store of his."

Mariah must have looked skeptical.

Emily Thurston Jamieson, who obviously knew something about management, proceeded to explain. "His father offered to invest in the store," she said. "But that meant his father had a lot of ideas about how the store should be run. Probably good ideas," she added. "But Teague wanted to do it on his own."

Emily waited, perhaps letting the implication sink in. Teague didn't want help any more than Mariah did.

"And," Emily continued, "he has done a remarkable job, considering."

"Considering?"

"He's a backcountry guide," Emily said. "And an excellent one, from what I've heard. But he's not a business person. He needs help."

Mariah wondered what Teague would think of getting advice from the former manager of the Thurston Hotel.

"He's been trying to get someone to do his accounting for ages."

"He has?"

"He hates that sort of thing."

"He does?"

"And management is in your blood."

"It is?"

Greta brought the tea. "I thought you'd like your

china," she said.

Emily's face glowed as she looked at *her china*. An elegant white china teapot with a polka dot pattern. The bottom half was pink, the top half white. Scatters of red roses mixed over the polka dots. A scrolled edge of gold trimmed the rim. The other dishes matched: a pitcher of cream, a covered sugar bowl, and the dessert plates.

"Thank you, Greta," Emily said. "This is lovely."

It made sense that Emily would get special treatment in the hotel. But Mariah never would have guessed that Emily would pick a pattern like this. The design was romantic and . . . something else . . . .

Playful? A different side of the pragmatic Mrs. Emily Thurston Jamieson.

But it wasn't only the dishes. Showcased with ripe raspberries, swirls of raspberry sauce and little dollops of whipped cream, the crème caramel looked scrumptious.

"Guy knows how to cook," Mariah said. "The hotel is fortunate to have him."

"Yes, we are," Emily said, pouring their tea.

For the next several minutes, the talk was only of flavors and presentations. Everything that was wrong with life was temporarily forgotten.

Emily set down her fork. "I really am sorry about your father," she said.

There it was again, that strange regret for someone she'd never known. Perhaps it had something to do with being old and sentimental.

"Thanks," Mariah said, "but it's okay. Really."

"Did your mother ever talk about him?"

"Sometimes, but not a lot, because it made her sad. I think she loved him very much."

Emily nodded. Kept quiet. For some reason, wanting to hear more.

"Obviously I never knew him." Mariah sipped her tea.

"When I was sixteen, I did go to see the rig, the one where he died." In her mind, she saw it again. The tall derrick, the seemingly random buildings, the big trucks, the roughnecks handling the pipe, the muddy ground.

"Someone saw me watching and offered me a hard hat so I could come closer," Mariah said, still seeing it in her mind. "But I didn't want to. And I never went back."

She took another slow sip of tea and let go of the image. "He's buried outside of Fort Mac. A little grave marker. That's all my mother could afford." Another sip of tea, full of the flavor of bergamot. "Some day when I have enough money, I want to get a bigger stone for him."

And then she snapped out of her reverie and looked across the table. "Emily? Is something wrong?"

Emily's normal peaches-and-cream complexion looked even whiter than usual. In fact, she looked like she was about to cry.

At precisely that moment, they were interrupted.

"Mariah! I'm so glad you're back. Oh hello, Mrs. Jamieson." Tessa clutched the end of the table.

"Tessa?" Mariah stared at the maid. "You look exhausted."

"I am," Tessa said. "I had to work last night. I mean—I was up late last night, and—"

"How many rooms are left?" Emily asked. Gone was the paleness. A problem had come up and Emily's composure had resurfaced.

"One room," Tessa answered. "The honeymoon suite on the fourth floor. The bathroom is cleaned and the rugs are vacuumed, but it needs the rose petal treatment. The candles, the champagne. All that crap. I am so tired, I can't focus anymore."

"Don't worry, Tessa," Emily Thurston Jamieson said as she rose to her feet. "You go home and get some rest. Mariah and I will finish the room."

. . . . .

Teague studied the label on the bottle of Rickard's Red. Four o'clock was probably a bit early for a beer, but all was well at the store and he needed to find Mariah.

She was sensitive about anyone helping her. Good thing she hadn't figured out where all the trays of food were coming from. But he couldn't help it. It wasn't that she needed taking care of. It was just that he couldn't resist.

Jason busied himself behind the bar, arranging bottles, polishing glasses.

"Figured out why she looks familiar?" Teague asked.

"No," Jason said. "I may have to ask Mrs. A."

"Mrs. Arbuckle?"

"She's the one who sent me to the bus depot last Thursday. The day your girlfriend arrived. I was supposed to pick her up."

But fate had intervened and Jason had left before Mariah had stepped off the bus.

She hadn't wanted any help then either, Teague remembered. Not your typical female. She was incredibly independent for such a little waif.

"Mrs. A said I would recognize her," Jason said. "And I do. I just can't remember how."

. . . . .

Mariah quickly changed out of her cable knit sweater into a light T-shirt. And then Mariah and Emily found Tessa's cart outside Room 47. There was no *Do Not Disturb* sign on the door, so hopefully the coast was clear.

Working quickly, they brought in a new bottle of champagne, added ice to the silver bucket and fresh water to the roses.

In the bathroom, Mariah set out new votive candles and

fresh towels. Emily opened the lavender bubbling bath salts and sprinkled about a cupful into the tub. "We are getting the orange scented ones." She sprinkled a bit more. "But I'm not using those for this honeymoon couple. They deserve the lavender."

"You're funny," Mariah said.

"I'm feeling a little vindictive." Emily capped the bottle. "Then again, that man was not good enough for you."

"No," Mariah agreed. "He wasn't."

"Teague is."

Mariah was not discussing Teague. "Giving advice again?"

"Sorry," Emily said. And then, "How do you like working with Tessa?"

Tessa? That was probably Emily trying to switch topics. And maybe trying to get a sense of the hotel staff.

"I like working with Tessa," Mariah said. "She's a hard worker. She does her job well and she's an excellent teacher."

Emily set the bottle of bath salts in the maid tray. "What do you mean by excellent?"

Folding her arms, Mariah leaned on the counter, and thought a moment.

"She shows you what to do, she lets you do it and then she finds something you did well, and she compliments you."

"So she's encouraging?"

"Yes."

"And then does she tell you what you did wrong?"

"No," Mariah said. "I already know what I did wrong. Tessa focuses on what I did right."

"Hmmm." Emily considered. "I like that."

"We're done here." Mariah picked up the tray of supplies. "Now the sheets."

Back in the main room, Emily pulled all the sheets off

the bed with one sweep.

Mariah waved out a contour sheet. "Are you happy retiring?"

"Yes, I think I am," Emily answered. She stuffed the used sheets into the hamper. "I'll always dabble but I trust Ben. He's a good manager."

Mariah fitted a corner of the contour sheet. Emily pulled it tight on the other side. They did the same for the other end. Next came the top sheet. Standing on either side of the bed, they pulled the top sheet up. But—

"Emily? What are you doing? This is the top of the bed."

"I know." She smiled, conspiratorially. "Help me tuck it in."

Together they stretched a large portion of the top sheet under the top of the mattress. So it looked like the top sheet was the bottom sheet.

Then Emily pulled the bottom of the sheet to the top, folding it in half. "Haven't you ever short-sheeted a bed?"

Mariah wanted to laugh but felt torn. "I . . . I don't think Bailey is going to like this."

"I don't care."

And, right at that moment, neither did Mariah. "Fine by me!" And who knew the old manager could be so much fun?

The comforter went on next, the folded sheet crisply fell over the edge of the comforter. Then the pillows were arranged. And then the rose petals.

"It's pretty," Emily said.

"Yes, it is," Mariah agreed. And they both sputtered with laughter.

Mariah aimed the cart toward the door. "We'd better get out of here before we get caught."

Emily held the door, and as Mariah pushed the cart through, she saw the old gentleman from the bus.

With his gold-rimmed spectacles perched on his nose, he wore his usual outfit. The navy blue sports jacket and the pale blue, striped shirt with the button down collar. Judging by the crispness of the collar, it was freshly laundered. Again.

He stood next to the supply closet across from Room 47—the supply closet, with the door open. From down the hall, they heard the elevator ding.

He pointed to the closet.

"Is that them?" Mariah asked him.

The old gentleman nodded, a big grin on his face.

"Quick!" Mariah said. "Into the closet!"

"What about the cart?" Emily asked.

"Leave it! They're coming!"

. . . . .

Teague knocked on the door of Suite One.

Since Jason had said Mrs. Arbuckle knew who Mariah was, Teague would talk to the old woman. He wasn't sure what he would say, but anything she might tell him could be helpful. And, for once in his life, he was going to ask for advice.

"Mr. Farraday! Come in. I was expecting you."

"You were?" He glanced around, looking for the little dog. Nowhere in sight.

"Gill is taking Betty Jo for a walk," Mrs. Arbuckle told him. "Let me get my shawl. It's a bit chilly. That's what I love about Septembers." She left him in her living room and bustled off to her bedroom.

Had Jason phoned ahead to say Teague was coming up? He hadn't told Jason what he was doing, but the bartender must have guessed.

Smart man.

Mrs. Arbuckle was taking her time. Either she was

having trouble finding her shawl, or she had more than one and she was deciding which one to take. While he waited, Teague studied the room. A pretty room—if you liked white everything. Walls, furniture, drapes. It would be a pain to keep clean. But then, Mrs. Arbuckle would not be the one cleaning it.

Wandering over to the fireplace, he looked down at the flames dancing on the grate. He liked fireplaces. And he liked campfires. There was something soothing about watching the flames ebb and glow. He had a feeling Mariah would like watching the flames too. Either a campfire, or sitting in front of the little fireplace in his apartment. Assuming he could make things right with her.

His attention fell on the mantel, on a small photograph with a shiny gold frame—a picture of an old man.

He had a ruddy complexion and laugh lines around his eyes. He was bald on top, but with a neatly trimmed ring of white hair. White hair, but very dark eyebrows, and a salt and pepper mustache. The picture showed him in a navy blue sports jacket with a pale blue shirt, open at the collar. Gold-rimmed glasses perched on the end of his nose, making him look wise.

Teague heard the door close behind him and then Mrs. Arbuckle was standing next to him.

"That's my Walter," she said.

"Your husband." He'd heard they had been very much in love for their whole marriage. "You must miss him."

"Oh, he's close." Mrs. Arbuckle pressed her hand over her heart. "Now we'd better get going."

"Going? Where?"

"Two floors down," she said. "The fun is about to start."

· · · · ·

"I don't hear anything, do you?" Emily asked, as she pressed her ear against the door.

Suddenly, they both heard a muffled roar. Someone suitably frustrated. The door across the hall clunked open, no sound for a second, and then the door slammed shut.

Mariah and Emily high-fived, started laughing again, and tried to stop, since they still wanted to hide.

"I think he thought you'd be in the hall," Emily whispered.

"Do you suppose he's calling downstairs?" Mariah asked. "If he tells Bailey, I'll say it was me. I don't want Tessa getting in trouble."

"I'll say it was both of us," Emily said.

"Why?"

"Because you need two people to properly short-sheet a bed."

"Of course you do." They erupted in giggles again.

"Maybe we should tiptoe out of here," Emily said. "We can take the stairwell up to Mrs. Arbuckle's suite."

"Listen." Mariah heard voices. "That's Teague. What's he doing up here?"

"And that's Maddie," Emily said. "Why would . . ."

"Mrs. Arbuckle? What are they doing here? Colby would not have called *them*."

"Shhh! Listen."

They pressed their ears to the door. More voices, different ones. Gill. And sure enough, Bailey. The door opened again with that loud chunking sound.

"Where is she!" Colby bellowed.

"Where is . . ." That was Bailey, trying to stall, probably hoping to smooth things over.

"Mariah! She did this!"

"Calm down, Mr. Clifford. What did she do?"

Emily opened the door and stepped out. "You silly man. Can't you take a joke?"

"Aunt Emily?" Bailey squeaked.

Mariah followed Emily out of the supply closet, and tried to look serious.

"I knew it was you!" Colby said, folding his arms and smirking.

"Aunt Emily? What's going on? You didn't—" A loud sigh. "All right. All of you, to my office. Now." Bailey narrowed a look at Teague. "Did you have anything to do with this?"

"I don't think so." He looked as calm and unfazed as ever.

Bailey huffed. "You might as well come too."

"I was coming anyway," he said.

· · · · ·

Once again, they were all together in Bailey's office.

Teague stood at the back, leaning against the wall. He felt curious about what was happening, and somewhat useless. A big part of him wanted to protect the little waif. Another part of him was pretty sure she knew how to protect herself. And that made him feel glad.

If somewhat useless.

Looking regal in her expensive red suit, Emily Jamieson sat in front of Bailey's desk with Mrs. Arbuckle on her left side, and Mariah on her right.

Somehow, even with her frayed jeans and her faded T-shirt, Mariah had that same regal quality as she sat there with her head high and her brilliant triumphant smile.

Could he ever hope to be part of her life?

Mariah and Emily kept bursting out in giggles. Mrs. Arbuckle, attempting to look dignified, pressed her lips together and glanced at the ceiling. No doubt trying to stop herself from joining the laughter.

After a few minutes, Bailey marched into her office and

Colby strutted after her. Rounding her desk, Bailey plopped into her chair. Colby followed her, coming to a stop beside her, acting as if he were in charge of this interview.

For someone with an axe to grind, he didn't look angry. Rather, he looked like a man bent on revenge, like a man who thought he had the upper hand. A man who probably rarely did.

"Olivia's not coming down?" Mariah asked, sweetly.

"She has had enough of you." Colby spat the words.

"I have had enough of her," Mariah said, simply.

"You are so irresponsible." Colby ranted. "You're never going to amount to anything. You should have stayed at the hospital. You had a decent job. You could have earned a decent living being a nurse. But no, not you. You had to go all weird."

"Weird?" Mrs. Arbuckle asked.

Colby ignored Mrs. Arbuckle and clamored on. "Your head nurse had to empty out the safety deposit box and sign the death certificate and deal with the funeral. You couldn't—or wouldn't—do any of it." He clenched his jaw. "Well, get over it. It's been almost three years. Move on!"

Three years? That's what Mariah had said, when they'd been at Boom Lake.

"Somebody died?" Mrs. Arbuckle asked, her brows knitted together.

"I am so glad I called off that wedding." Colby blustered away, carrying on with his monologue. "I would have been taking care of you forever while you dabbled with your stupid little business ideas." He paused, took a quick breath. "And now you're a maid. It figures."

"Who died?" Mrs. Arbuckle asked again.

"I want her fired from this hotel!" Colby shouted, stabbing his finger at Mariah.

Now the laughing was gone. Both Mariah and Emily focused on Colby, their expressions serious.

Colby turned to Bailey. "I'm meeting my wife in the Margaret Library. And when I come back here, I expect you to have fired this woman."

Mrs. Arbuckle stood up as Colby was exiting the office. "Young man. Stop right there," she commanded. "Tell me who died."

"You don't know?"

"Tell me."

"Mariah's mother," he said. "A car accident, three years ago. Icy roads. She was admitted to the ICU where Mariah worked. Her mother was there for a while. Before she died."

"Ten days," Mariah said, quietly.

"Yeah, for a few days. And Mariah quit. Sure, it was tough. I get it. But it was no reason to quit a perfectly good job." He glared at her. "Quit trying to pretend you'll ever get a business degree. You're not cut out for it."

Satisfied with his performance, he left the office. Silence fell, for about ten seconds, and then Teague said, "That's a sadly misguided take on reality."

"Emily?" Mariah stood beside Emily and clamped her fingers to Emily's wrist, checking her pulse.

"Aunt Emily?" Bailey got to her feet. "Mrs. Arbuckle, call Dr. Sheridan. I think she's having another heart attack."

"No," Emily said, her voice weak. A long, slow breath. "No," she repeated, a stronger voice this time. "All of you sit down and be quiet." She looked up at Mariah. "Three years ago?"

"Yes," Mariah said, letting go of Emily's wrist. "This November, it will be three years."

"I had a feeling I would never see her again," Emily said.

Mariah squinted, puzzled. She leaned over Emily again, to take her wrist. And as she did, her medallion slipped out from under her T-shirt and swung between them.

Emily reached out and touched it, carefully holding the antique gold in her fingers, turning the amethyst so it sparkled in the overhead light.

And then she started to cry.

"Is that what I think it is?" Bailey asked, in a voice filled with awe.

"Yes. It is," Emily said. "The Thurston Heirloom."

A ruckus in the hallway had them all turning toward the door as an irate Colby stomped back into the room.

"Can somebody tell me why you people have a picture of Mariah in your library!"

Epilogue

Three weeks later . . .

The yellow needles of the larch glowed all around them in the warm September sunshine. The intense blue sky contrasted with the new snow on the high mountain peaks. Late season wildflowers—asters and pine drops and gentians—lifted and stirred in the light breeze.

Teague sat with Mariah on a rock outcropping overlooking the valley. He watched as Gill spread the picnic blanket and set up camp chairs for Emily and Zach, Teague's grandfather.

Zach Farraday had wanted to come on the Larch Valley hike and the two seniors seemed to be hitting it off, chatting and laughing as they unpacked the lunch Chef Guy had prepared especially for the Thurston Hotel's former manager.

"I thought you said this would be crowded."

"It usually is. But it's Monday. The crowds are lighter."

They sat in silence for a time, listening to the mountains. Mariah had called them guardians. Guardians who watched over the world, who put everything into perspective, and who made everything right.

He didn't know if it was the guardians or fate, but he felt like everything was right. Like his life was full.

"Do you want me to go with you to Fort Mac?"

She thought about it. "No."

"Yeah, I didn't think so."

"Another time," Mariah said. "Emily and I will make this trip. Just the two of us."

"It's a pilgrimage for her."

"Yes, and she wants to pay for the new gravestones for my parents."

Teague heard the hesitancy in Mariah's voice. "You don't like taking her money."

"No."

"Whatever she doesn't spend on you now, you'll inherit."

"I hope that's a long time away," Mariah said, wistfully. "I like having a grandmother."

Mariah didn't need anyone's money. She had her very own Trust Fund. It had been sitting there ever since Emily and Michael Jamieson had set up an irrevocable trust for their lost daughter, Mary, and any children she might have. On top of that Mariah would someday inherit Emily's wealth and interest in the hotel. His little waif had turned out to be independently wealthy.

Teague could still remember the sick look on Colby Clifford's face when the guy realized he had dumped an heiress.

"You really do look like your great-grandmother," Teague said. He was surprised he'd never noticed the portrait before. But it wasn't like he was in the Margaret Library very often.

Jason also didn't spend a lot of time in the library, but that is where Jason had seen the portrait that looked so much like Mariah. The portrait of Margaret Thurston on her wedding day, wearing her hair up, and wearing the amethyst medallion.

"Margaret Thurston." Mariah leaned against his arm. "Did I tell you I have Margaret for a middle name?"

"No," he said, and then he tried out the name. "Mariah

Margaret Patrick. It has a nice ring to it." He thought for a moment. "But, I think Mariah Margaret Farraday sounds even better."

"I want my degree first," she said. "But keep proposing and one day I may say yes." She laughed. That sweet musical sound he loved so much.

With the trust fund, Mariah could attend university in person. Her newly found cousin, Ben, was encouraging her and helping her with her studies.

Her other cousin, Bailey, had moved her into a room on the fifth floor of the hotel. Bailey would have given her a suite on the sixth floor but Mariah had refused. She wanted the sixth floor suites for the "more important guests" of the Thurston.

Emily had even offered her recently vacated house. But Mariah said she liked living at the hotel. "It's more fun." It probably was, and not only that, there were many nights when Mariah was at Teague's apartment—which was definitely *more fun.*

"Emily is getting right into being a grandmother," he said.

"She is. She says she wants to relax and enjoy her granddaughter." Mariah paused. "That's me. I have a grandmother. It's still hard to believe."

"I bet Emily would like to enjoy some great-grandchildren too," Teague said.

"You don't give up, do you?"

"Just trying to help out." He kissed her. He was getting used to kissing her and he figured he would do it for the rest of his life.

"And," he said, "I'll say it again. I don't want any help from you. I don't care how much money you have in that Trust Fund of yours."

"I know." She smiled and tilted her head. "But those books need doing, and I seem to remember you telling me

. . . *You can do it on your own, but it's nice to have help?* Is that how you put it?"

He sighed. "I guess."

Mariah did her course work from Tuesday to Thursday. She handled his accounting on Mondays and Fridays. The red and green bear bells were selling out.

Monroe liked working with Mariah, handling customers, and organizing merchandise. And Shredder was happy to be out of sales and doing guiding full time.

Like now.

"Hey, Boss!" Shredder called from down the hill. "Lunch is ready!"

BOOKS IN THE THURSTON HOTEL SERIES

Find them all at www.ThurstonHotelBooks.com

With Open Arms
Book 6
by M. K. Stelmack

The Starlight Garden
Book 7
by Maeve Buchanan

Betting On Courage
Book 8
by Alyssa Linn Palmer

The Thurston Heirloom
Book 9
by Suzanne Stengl

An Angel's Secret
Book 10
by Ellen Jorgy

To A Tea
Book 11
by Katie O'Connor

A Thurston Christmas
Book 12
by Brenda Sinclair

Also by Suzanne Stengl

On the Way to a Wedding

Ryder O'Callaghan finds Toria Whitney on the side of a forest road with a totaled car, a sprained ankle, and a wedding dress. Both Ryder and Toria are scheduled to be married in three weeks—but not to each other.

Angel Wings

Her angel has arrived. His mission is to accompany her to the wedding. And to prepare for it, she must complete three tasks . . .

The Ghost and Christie McFee

A new diver, an underwater town, two ghosts—

About the Author

I've been telling stories since I was a child. Then, it was stories about fairies and mermaids, told to my sisters when we were supposed to be sleeping. As a teenager, I wrote long diary entries and I wrote short pieces of fiction—that no one but me ever read.

Don't get me wrong, I was not a total recluse. I did lots of "real world" things too. I became a nurse, I spent time with friends, I traveled a lot. And I always wrote.

Sometimes after a difficult day at work, I would recreate the day in a story that had a better ending. That's still what I do—I create stories with happy, hopeful endings.

"Suzanne Stengl has a lovely voice with a subtle hint of humor."
—*A.M. Westerling, author of A Knight for Love*

"Suzanne Stengl's descriptions and characters are really memorable."
—*Amy Jo Fleming, author of Death at Bandit Creek*

Find more books by Suzanne Stengl at
www.suzannestengl.com

If you enjoyed The Thurston Heirloom
you can help others find this story
by leaving a short review on Amazon.

CPSIA information can be obtained
at www.ICGtesting.com
Printed in the USA
LVOW12s0218051017
551235LV00001B/18/P